I couldn't see his eyes—his green rhinestone sunglasses hid them—but he stared at me as if *I* were the one in drag as a Baltimore Hon. His feet were stuffed awkwardly into pink mules with fluffy toe pieces. I started to laugh, but he didn't. He just stared at me, so long that I turned to see if someone else was standing behind me. There was no one.

Feeling flirty and free in this city where I knew no one and no one knew me, I smiled and waved the end of my boa. I felt giddy with girl power, as if I had cast a spell on this guy who couldn't stop staring at me. He suddenly came to his senses, turned and walked on, but his eyes—his sunglasses—strayed back to me.

Summer in the City

ELIZABETH CHANDLER

AVON BOOKS
An Imprint of HarperCollins *Publishers*

Summer in the City
Copyright © 2006 by Mary Claire Helldorfer
For information address HarperCollins
Children's Books, a division of HarperCollins
Publishers, 1350 Avenue of the Americas, New
York, NY 10019.
www.harperteen.com

Library of Congress Catalog Card Number:
2005906568
ISBN-10: 0-06-084734-4
ISBN-13: 978-0-06-084734-0

Typography by Jennifer Bankenstein
❖
First Avon edition, 2006

To Carla,
who graciously allowed me
to "redecorate" her home,
and Monalisa,
who lent her name and open spirit.

Summer
in
the
City

Chapter 1

"They're dancing really close, Jamie."

I nodded, unable to tear my eyes from the couple spinning slowly beneath the ballroom chandelier.

"I think his arms are Krazy Glued to her back," Mike added.

"Looks like it," I muttered, wondering how I could be the last to know about this.

"They're dancing really, really slow," said Ron, who was standing on the other side of me.

"Well, the *music* is slow," I pointed out.

"Dance any slower, and they're going to stop and make out."

"Ron, please!" I hissed.

But it didn't matter if anyone else overheard my two escorts and me talking. Everyone at the senior prom had already noticed. The lineup of faculty and chaperoning parents had their eyes fixed on the couple.

"Do you think old Rupert's going to break it up?" Mike asked.

Ron snorted, and I imagined our vice principal hauling the couple off the dance floor, lecturing them in the coat-check room. But the truth was, they weren't doing anything off-limits. Maybe that was what fascinated me. They gave a whole new meaning to the word *romantic*, showing the rest of us, who went from a clumsy version of slow dancing to a clumsy version of stuff that *was* off-limits—in about fifteen seconds—to be total amateurs.

I watched the guy who, earlier in the evening, had gazed at me in my green, strapless gown, and said, "My God, who is this beautiful woman?"

I watched the one guy who'd always made me feel good about myself, the one guy I could count on whenever I had a problem, looking at someone else as if she were his whole world, as if he wanted to ride off into the sunset with her.

Well, after this prom was over, he and I were going to have a talk, a good, long talk.

I just hoped he made it home before I did. It's embarrassing when your dad has a better time at your prom than you.

At six A.M., with Mike curled up and sleeping like a six-foot-five baby in the back seat of the car, Ron walked me to the front door. "You're the best, Jamie," Ron said.

"Yeah, thanks, it was fun," I told him. "Good night—good morning—whatever."

And good-bye to the most disappointing high school dating career in Michigan, I thought. Well, that was an exaggeration—it's not like I had distinguished myself in that category. No, I had simply joined the very large club of high school girls who hoped things would be better in college. Some of those girls didn't go to our prom at all; some went with girlfriends; some went with guys they had dated forever and wondered why they had even bothered; and some, like me, got together with guys who were "just friends." I happened to have two "just friends" who couldn't face asking a real date to the prom, but being jocks, were too embarrassed to go with each other.

Walking to the front door, I noticed that Dad's car was missing from the driveway. I let myself into the silent house. Our rancher, one of the newer houses at the edge of our small Michigan town, was a place guys loved to hang out, with chip bowls instead of vases decorating the living room, sports trophies lining the fireplace mantel, and a big-screen TV facing a black leather sectional. There were smaller TVs on either side of the big screen, because sometimes great games are scheduled for the same time slot, and watching a game on tape just isn't the same. I have trouble remembering the way the place looked eight years ago, when my parents filed for divorce.

My mother loved me, and I loved her, but from the moment I was born, I was Dad's kid. I played every version of little league sports available to girls and tagged along with him to practices and games when he was a young coach teaching at the only high school in town, the one from which I was now graduating. It was natural that the guys who hung around Coach Carvelli's house, even as they gradually became my age, were great buddies with "Coach's kid." The fact that I could even off a pickup game—and was better than some of the guys my dad coached—was a big plus. For *them*.

Something had happened to me in the last two years. No, not hormones—those kicked in at the beginning of middle school when I first started noticing more about Dad's players than their game stats. In some ways it would have been a lot easier if I could have said to my girl-friends, who think that I am lucky to hang around a lot of guy jocks, "I am so freakin' frus-trated by all these turkeys who want to be just friends. I want sex." I mean, everybody is sup-posed to want that, right? But what I wanted was a whole lot more and a whole lot harder to come by: romance. Judging from the way the other girls at the prom were watching Dad and Miss Matlock, wrapped in each other's arms, off in a world of their own, maybe romance wasn't an easy thing for any of us to come by—even those who didn't stand six feet tall in their glittery stocking feet.

I looked down, then peeled off my sparkling panty hose and draped them on this year's trophy for All-Regional Girls Athlete, front and center over the fireplace. Outside, a car door closed quietly. I had left the front door open, so Dad knew I was home and awake. It seemed to me he took an unusually long time to walk from our driveway to the house.

"Oh, hello," he said, trying to look surprised to see me. I saw myself in the reflection of our big-screen TV, standing stiffly with my arms folded, my blonde hair a tangled mess, looking like a parent who had been kept up way too long.

"Have a good time?" I asked.

"Wonderful," he said. "And you?"

"Okay," I replied.

"Join me for an orange juice?" he asked, and I followed him into the kitchen.

We sat across from each other at the kitchen table, as we had a million times before. Even in the morning light, the rental tux worked its magic, making him look at least ten years younger than fifty-one, which was still a good ten years older than Miss Matlock, I figured.

"So you and Miss Matlock have been see-ing each other," I said.

"Well, we see each other at school every day, of course," he weaseled.

"You know what I mean, Dad."

"Yes, I know what you mean. I'd wondered if you'd noticed that I wasn't always at home or practice."

I had, and I had even noticed him standing in the school halls talking to Miss Matlock, seeming very interested in what she said. But since she was our junior–senior guidance coun-selor, and Dad was always working to get his athletes well placed in colleges, I had chalked up their conversations to that. Or to me — we had started scouting out women's athletic schol-arships the end of my sophomore year. Naturally he'd talk to my guidance counselor. It had never occurred to me that he might be planning for the future of someone other than his ath-letes or me.

As for him being out a lot more than usual, I had been so grateful for the privacy, so glad for the opportunity to turn off ESPN and click on a romantic DVD, I hadn't given much thought to what he was up to. Besides, if I'd asked Dad where he was those evenings, he might have asked me what game I'd been watching, which was the last thing I wanted. Dad and I didn't talk about feelings—except those connected to the thrill of winning and the agony of defeat. I could never have admitted to him that I had started reading the kinds of books Mom liked—the kinds of books Mom *wrote*.

As if Dad had just read my mind, he said, "You're almost eighteen, Jamie, ready to go off to college. I guess it stands to reason that we both have secrets."

But your secret is a woman, I wanted to argue, and mine is a novel by Nora Roberts hidden beneath the cover of *Competing in a Triathlon*.

The mature part of me triumphed. "I'm glad you found someone, Dad. You deserve some good things coming your way, besides championship titles."

I meant it. He could hear it in my voice and took from that some encouragement. "I've asked Christine to join us at the cabin this summer."

"You've—what?!"

"I'm sure you can understand, Jamie," he rushed on. "With her schedule and mine, practice every afternoon, games on nights and weekends, and so many eyes watching us, it's hard. We want to see . . . to see if it will work."

By *it* he meant a permanent pairing of them, I supposed.

"What better place than our cabin?"

I could think of a lot of better places. This house, for instance, next September, when I was gone. Couldn't he wait three more months? Yes, I was being selfish. "And where am I supposed to go?" I asked.

"To the cabin," he replied with surprise, sounding a little hurt to think I'd do otherwise. "Jamie, it wouldn't be the same without you. You know I wouldn't want it any other way."

"And does Miss Matlock know that?"

"I explained it all to her."

"Did you explain what we do up there?" Basically, we fished, we hiked, and we watched sports TV; then we fished, we hiked, and we watched sports TV. Actually, last year, for the first time in my life, I had started to think it was pretty boring.

"Oh, yes. She sees it as an adventure."

I didn't know Miss Matlock well, but I had always assumed her adventures took place in shoe stores. "Does she know that there isn't a mall within a hundred miles of the cabin?"

"Well, I don't think I went into that kind of detail."

You should have, I thought, but that was his problem. Mine was to get over the fact that this summer, which I was suddenly getting very sentimental about, was going to be radically different.

"It will be terrific, Jamie. I'm sure of it. The three of us will—"

I held up my hand, recognizing from his tone of voice the beginning of one of Coach Carvelli's teamwork talks. "Dad, I'm really tired. And nothing seems terrific when you're tired, except sleeping."

He nodded sympathetically, although he was wide awake, his eyes bright and skin pinkish. He was feeling like a kitten in May. "We can talk later," he said.

For the next two hours I tossed and turned in bed. Did Mom know about Miss Matlock?

Months of conference calls had preceded the joint decision for me to attend the University of Maryland. I had always assumed that my parents had private discussions about finances; did they talk about more personal things—like who they were dating? Was that why Mom told me I was welcome to spend the summer with her and get to know Maryland a little better? No, she said something like that every year.

I dozed off and dreamed of "Chrissy," as the kids at school sarcastically referred to Miss Matlock, fishing at the end of our dock, swinging her happy feet in a pair of high-heeled flip-flops. She was so touchy-feely and enthusiastic about everything. Why did Dad have to pick *her*? I woke up even grumpier than before.

Finally, at two in the afternoon, with sun streaming into my room, but my head lost in that weird twilight that hovers around you when you've been awake virtually twenty-four hours, I picked up the phone and punched in a long-distance number.

"Hello, Mom?"

Chapter 2

On the second Friday in June, I rolled down the windows of my old Camry, pumped up my CD player, and headed for the interstate. For the last several days, Miss Matlock had been bustling around our house, chirping like a sparrow, helping Dad pack for summer at the cabin. I couldn't drive away fast enough.

I sang at the top of my lungs my first hour on the highway. During the second hour, I hummed. By the third hour, I had the car's AC blowing and I was sipping rest-stop cappuccino, quietly listening to my music. Slipping in with my favorite songs were a million high school memories. Thoughts of friends and teammates, coaches and teachers, began to take over. Every time I thought of Dad, I got a large lump in my throat. For thirty awful minutes I drove gripping the steering wheel, slowing down and looking at exit ramps where I might get off and turn around. But I kept going.

When I got to the small motel where my parents had insisted that I stop for the night, I discovered that each of them had called the desk four times to find out if I had arrived. The lump in my throat disappeared. So much for being on my own!

The next morning I started out singing again, then got sentimental again, then got something else—nervous. I knew no one in Baltimore. I had never spent summer in a city. Until her move in January, my mother hadn't lived in Baltimore since she was a kid.

After my parents split in Michigan, Mom taught middle school in a rural town in Maryland that was similar to ours in Michigan, so I had always felt comfortable visiting her, as comfortable as I could be in rooms where everything was edged in ruffles or lace. Now that I was about to turn eighteen and start a whole new life in college—one that I secretly hoped would include romance—I wanted my parents to act the way they had always acted. I wanted them to be old and stable, boring if necessary. Instead, Dad was behaving like a sixteen-year-old in love and Mom was hurling herself headlong into her second career—as a writer of romance novels.

I arrived in Baltimore, turning into an old neighborhood called Hampden, around one o'clock Saturday. Apparently, everyone else had arrived at twelve thirty, for cars were jammed nose to tail along street after street of skinny townhouses—"row houses," Mom called them. She had sent me a map with a note saying that something called HonFest was going on. After grabbing a space three blocks from her house, I decided to leave my boxes of stuff in the car and followed her map to Chestnut Avenue.

A note was taped to her front door:

> *Jamie,*
> *I'm signing books. Look for the pink*
> *flamingo on The Avenue. My table*
> *is in front of Hometown Girl.*
> *Love,*
> *Mom*

She had attached a festival map and circled her location. Before dealing with the fuss my mother always made when she first saw me, I decided to explore the place where she had chosen to live out her dream.

The houses—most of them made of brick or covered with some weird brown-and-gray stone that was obviously fake—were narrow and long, stretching way back to the yards and alleys behind them. Hanging flower baskets, sculptures made from hubcaps and bike parts, statues of St. Francis and the Blessed Mother, and pink flamingos decorated the tiny lawns and porches. I wandered down 36th Street, a street of storefronts and houses turned into stores, also called "The Avenue," pausing to look in a shop called Fat Elvis. Tackiness seemed to be an art form here.

Some of the crowd that swarmed the closed-off blocks of Hampden's main street were dressed for heat and humidity. But there was a guy in a red, rhinestone-decorated Elvis outfit, and women of all ages with huge, teased-out hair—beehives. The beehive ladies wore cat's-eye glasses, red lipstick, and stretchy print pants.

Scarves and feathery boas floated around bare shoulders as they strutted on their spiky heels. Big ball earrings swung from their ears. Nearly all of the women and girls carried fantastic purses. They were "Baltimore Hons"— I realized, after reading a festival poster with photos from last year's Best Hon contest. My mother had said the festival celebrated working-class women and life in the 50s, a period which, apparently, had lasted a very long time in Hampden.

My mother had warned me to come prepared for heat. Even in my spaghetti-strap shirt and shorts, I was sweating. I bought a large sparkly clip from a booth and pulled my hair up in a loose ponytail, then purchased a bright pink boa. It was too light to make me hot and felt very girly as it drifted around my shoulders. *Maybe this is my summer to try out* really *girly,* I thought, as I worked my way down the Avenue, carefully circumventing the area where my mother would be signing books. The pink flamingo she had mentioned couldn't be missed, stretching two stories high and attached to a fire escape on the front of a building.

I was just starting to get hungry when I came upon a parked bus painted to look like a monstrous blue can of Spam. I lost my appetite when I realized people were standing around eating Spam burgers. Next to the bus, kids were bowling, rolling small balls down an alley, trying to knock over stacked cans of Spam. I felt as if I had landed on an alien planet. Why hadn't my mother chosen New York—didn't writers go there?

But then I saw a group of great-looking guys waiting for their chance to bowl, wolfing down the disgusting burgers, laughing and joking and being loud. With them was a Baltimore Hon, a girl as tall as I—check that, a guy! I saw it by the way he wobbled on his high-heeled mules as he crumpled up his drink cup and strode toward a trash can. I watched, smiling to myself, and at that moment, he became aware of me studying him and turned to look back.

I couldn't see his eyes—his green rhinestone sunglasses hid them—but he stared at me as if *I* were the one in drag as a Baltimore Hon. My eyes dropped to his stretchy leopard-print pants, which clung to extremely muscular legs.

His feet were stuffed awkwardly into pink mules with fluffy toe pieces. I started to laugh, but he didn't. He just stared at me, so long that I turned to see if someone else, like Fat Elvis, was standing behind me. There was no one.

Feeling flirty and free in this city where I knew no one and no one knew me, I smiled and waved the end of my boa. I felt giddy with girl power, as if I had cast a spell on this guy who couldn't stop staring at me. He suddenly came to his senses, turned, and walked on, but his eyes—his sunglasses—strayed back to me.

"Hey, hon, watch where you're going!" one of his friends yelled, but the guy had his eyes on me. He tripped over the street curb. Trying to catch his balance, unsteady on his high heels, he staggered wildly, then sprawled across the pavement. When he sat up next to the trash can, his red beehive wig sat cockeyed on his head. He snatched up his sunglasses, shoving them back on his face as if to keep people from recognizing him. His friends howled with laughter. The guy whirled around and hurled both fluffy pink shoes at them, realizing too late that it made him look like a girl throwing a hissy fit. Now his friends roared louder and others joined in.

The guy grabbed up his boa with a fierceness that made a flurry of feathers. I pressed the back of my hand against my mouth, but I was shaking with laughter. A big satin rose had tumbled out of his wig, and when he bent over in his leopard pants to retrieve it, it wasn't a pretty sight. A second rose that had been catapulted from his wig had rolled toward me. I picked it up, but the guy was obviously avoiding further glances in my direction, and I wasn't sure what to do with it.

"Excuse me," I called softly, as if it were possible to get only his attention.

His friends grinned at me—leered may have been a more accurate word. They realized that I was the one who had distracted him.

"Hi, hon," one of them called to me. "What's your name?"

Now I became self-conscious and was no more willing than the guy-Hon to cross the twenty-five feet between us.

"Look, your little sweetie has your rose," one of his friends told him.

Despite the guy's tan, I could see his

cheeks coloring. Mine burned as well—"*little sweetie*"—what was that supposed to mean? The guys had that cocky jock look and were eyeing my extra long legs in an obvious, obnoxious way.

The Hon glanced over at me. I threw the rose at him like a strike through the heart of home plate, then hurried off in the opposite direction.

"Baby!" my mother greeted me.

"Hey, Mom."

"Everyone, this is my baby, Jamie. Isn't she beautiful?"

Two middle-aged women, a woman grasping the hand of an antsy little kid, and a girl not much older than me smiled and murmured agreement. What else were they going to do—they were waiting in line for her autograph.

"*Very* beautiful," said the man sitting next to my mother at the signing table.

"Jamie, this is Viktor."

Light-haired, blue-eyed, and thirty-something, Viktor rose to shake my hand. *Whoa*, I thought, *is this what romance publishers look like?*

Then I remembered: Mom called her editor Priscilla.

"It's a pleasure to meet you," Viktor said, in an accent that I thought was Swedish. He had a body perfect for modeling skimpy gym wear. Maybe he did publicity for the chick-lit line, I thought—clever marketing!

"I've got a half hour more here, baby. Would you like the house key?"

"No, I'll get something to eat and hang out."

"Get the crab cakes," she said, pulling bills from a blue alligator purse as kitschy as those that some of the Hons were carrying.

"I've got money, thanks."

I left Mom to her fans, but when I was about thirty feet away, I turned back to look at her, trying to see her the way a stranger would. We had the same green eyes, and the same hair, although hers, dyed now, was a paler yellow than my streaky blond. Standing just five foot five and sporting some big curves, wearing her hair and bangs too long for a woman who was fifty, she looked like a country western singer— or a romance writer, I reminded myself. I watched a woman clutching one of Mom's books to her breast, talking animatedly. Mom was radiant—she had found her dream.

Then I saw Viktor watching me watch Mom. His smile was slow and confident and revealed perfectly even, white teeth. Feeling uncomfortable, I moved on.

I found a booth selling crab cakes, and carried my sandwich and iced tea to an area in front of the festival's main stage, choosing a seat in the last row. Up front, members of a school band with a color guard were wiping sweat off their faces. Hons of all ages were gathering, some of them practicing their poses, getting ready for the big contest. I scanned the group for my guy-Hon, but he wasn't there.

By the time I finished the crab cake, the heat and long drive from Michigan had caught up with me. Feeling pleasantly sleepy, I shut my eyes, soaking up the June sunlight, and thought about "my" Hon. Since he obviously wasn't enjoying his day in drag, I figured he was being initiated into some group. I wondered what he looked like without the wig and makeup, what kinds of things he liked to do, what his voice sounded like.

"You're desperate, Jamie," I told myself, "when you have romantic thoughts about a guy in high heels." Still, I tried to imagine what would make him smile and how his laughter sounded. . . .

I woke up with a start, awakened by a clash of cymbals during the National Anthem. Realizing that I was the only one sitting, I rose hastily to my feet. Something rolled off my lap. I picked up a pink satin rose, the one I had thrown back at my Hon. Quickly I looked around, but he was nowhere in sight.

I studied the rose, then attached it to my shirt, wrapping its wire base around my strap. The rose was old, which made it seem as if it had once been special to someone. I touched its fabric gently, lovingly. Dropping it in my lap was the most romantic thing a guy had ever done for me.

Chapter 3

"*WE WANT TURTLE SOUP*," I read from a sign that hung in a window that may have been Mom's or may have belonged to the house next door. It was hard to tell. The series of houses that grew out of the pavement on Chestnut Avenue had one long Formstone front that appeared to ripple, with two windows bowing out, followed by a flat area for an entrance, the pattern repeating itself over and over down the block.

Mom laughed. "Three boys from Hopkins University rent that house, although only two are here this summer. Hopkins has a great lacrosse team, and their rival is your new team, the Maryland Terrapins—turtles. We'll have to get one of those signs that reads *FEAR THE TURTLE* to hang in *our* window. You're going to like this town, baby. Sports are big."

So Dad had said, right after he explained rather sheepishly that he had signed me up for a lacrosse camp at a local high school. The camp's brochure had photographs of an exclusive private school and promoted its program as "excellent for girls with the potential to tap athletic scholarships to Ivy League colleges." Dad had tried to get me into a college camp, but I didn't have the game experience required. I had played only one-on-one with Dad. Apparently, in Maryland, where he grew up, they started lacrosse at the age of three.

"Well, come on in," Mom said. Viktor and I followed her, each of us carrying two cartons of clothes from my car. I wondered when Viktor would change out of his revealing cropped T-shirt and skintight jeans into something more comfortable and hop his train back to New York.

"Why don't I fix us something cool and healthy to drink?" he suggested.

"Wonderful idea!" my mother replied, setting down my overnight bag, then waving her hands around the living room. "Well . . . how do you like it?"

I glanced around. The room had mauve walls and a high ceiling with a fan whose paddles were shaped and painted like palm leaves. Lace curtains hung from the windows that bowed out to the street and stretched almost from ceiling to floor. Festoons of gaudy artificial flowers draped the top of them and hung along their sides. A gray velvet sofa and chair were smothered in shiny purple-and-pink pillows. The silk shades of two floor lamps were lilac-colored and fringed. A third lamp dangled little crystals. Candles lined the mantel of the fake fireplace, their fragrance so strong it made my eyes water. There were flowers there, too, bouquets of them stuffed around the candles, and my graduation photo, framed in a heart, looked like it sat on an altar. It was the tackiest, girliest room I had ever seen.

"Nice," I said.

"Wait till you see the rest!" my mother responded happily.

"Maybe she wants to see the bathroom first, Rita," Viktor said. "Upstairs, down the hall, nearly at the end."

He met the surprise in my eyes with a slow-spreading smile. He had said that on purpose. People who easily described where the bathroom was spent a lot of time in a place—he wasn't hopping a train to anywhere.

I looked quickly at Mom.

"I'll get the drinks," said Viktor.

"Mom?" I asked, when he had disappeared through the series of rooms that made up her long narrow house.

"Yes?" she said, trying to look as if she had no idea what I was going to ask.

"Who is he?"

"You'll like him, Jamie. He's athletic like you. He works as a personal trainer."

"*Your* personal trainer?"

She blushed a little. "I'm one of his clients. He works at my health club."

"I see." Oh, did I see, and this time, there was no place to run. I had rejected Dad and Chrissy the Counselor; now I was stuck with Mom and Viktor the Studly Swede. But wasn't I the one turning eighteen? Wasn't it *my* turn for romance?

"Would you like to use the bathroom?" my mother asked, sounding almost apologetic.

"I guess so." Now that I was prepared for

shaving cream on the sink, why not?

My mother picked up my overnight bag and I followed her, carrying two cartons of clothes, struggling to get up a set of steps that ran behind the living room and were just wide enough to allow me to keep my elbows.

I glimpsed a bedroom to the left that emitted a kind of pink glow, and turned right down a narrow hall. Mom entered the room at the end of the hall and set down my bag. "You'll be sleeping in my office," she said. "The bathroom is right next door."

"Your office! Mom, you don't want me in your work space." But she didn't want me in her bedroom, either, I realized, for that was crowded enough. "I thought you had three bedrooms."

"I do, but the middle one is full of boxes."

"Well, how about the basement?"

"I guess you've never been in the basement of an old city house," my mother replied. "I have a laptop, Jamie, and really, I move all over the place. I just keep my things here. The daybed is very comfy."

The daybed was covered with a leopard-print spread, and the two windows, which looked out the back of the house, had leopard-print valances. The walls were lime green. I figured the furry black-and-white striped pillows were supposed to be zebra skins and touched them gingerly.

"Like it, baby?"

"It's, uh, kind of jungle-y."

She beamed. "That's exactly what I was aiming for, a little excitement, a stroll on the wild side."

"All right, wild women, your juices are ready," Viktor said, his voice startling me. He must have padded down the hall on panther paws.

Mom giggled up at him, then winked at me. I wondered if the Hopkins students next door would allow me to use their third room.

"I'll be down in minute, okay?"

"Sure, hon," said my mother, slipping into Baltimore talk.

I used the bathroom, which contained enough soaps, perfumes, and lotions to supply an entire women's dorm, then returned to my new room.

Doors had been removed from the double

closet opposite the back windows, and my mother used the area as a writing alcove, her desk chair facing in, the three walls lined with photographs of buildings and rooms on a Southern estate, floor plans, a town map, a calendar—the world of her latest novel, I realized. Post-its were stuck on her laptop, her walls, the edge of her desk, and on an area by the daybed, where she must have been sitting and thinking. I read some of the ideas and descriptions jotted on them; if someone had been looking over my shoulder, I would have blushed. Mom sure had a way with words.

In one corner of her room were three large frames with poster-size copies of the covers from her first three books. Big-bosomed women were being swept into the arms of iron-breasted men. I hadn't read her books; it's one thing to read Nora Roberts's plots of romance and lust, it's another to read your mother's.

Well, I couldn't hide up here forever. After checking out the middle bedroom, which was filled with large boxes, then my mother's bedroom, which glowed like a sunset, and which, to my relief, had a gym bag and shaving kit, suggesting that Mom's personal trainer stayed overnight but wasn't a full-time resident, I headed downstairs.

I found Viktor and Mom in the backyard, sipping some kind of healthy concoction he had made. A third frothy glass of reddish stuff waited for me.

Studying Viktor in the bright sunlight I could see that, while his body was probably twenty-five years younger than Mom's, his face was maybe just fifteen. Still, that was quite a difference in age, given that guys (my father, for instance) usually went for younger women.

I sipped the drink, which smelled like cabbage, then held the glass against my cheek, the cold concoction feeling a lot better than it tasted.

"Who would ever guess that vegetables could taste so good," my mother commented, swirling the cubes in her glass.

All I could think was, *If he's poisoning her, she'll never be able to tell.*

"So," said Viktor. "Your mother tells me you are a fabulous athlete."

"I'm good enough," I said.

"Baby, you won a full athletic scholarship to Maryland."

"What is your sport?" Viktor asked, as if he hadn't been studying my long legs the way I had been studying his skin in an effort to determine his age.

"Basketball."

"Maybe you would like some free passes to the Club," he said.

"The Club?"

"That would be lovely," Mom gushed. "We could work out together, Jamie."

I tried to picture the two of us side by side in stretchy little exercise outfits, the same face, one body short and curvy, the other tall and lean: We'd look like cartoon characters.

"Of course, you could come alone," Viktor told me. "I'll get you some passes. I'd be glad to design a regimen for you."

"I, uh, already have a regimen from my coach at Maryland," I replied.

"Oh? I'd be very interested in seeing it."

"What I mean is, she's sending me one. I

guess it hasn't come in the mail yet," I said to Mom.

"No, hon."

His slow, even smile told me Viktor knew I was lying. He glanced at his watch. "I should be going, Rita," he said, his accent making her name distinct. "Stay where you are, my lovely, I'll get my things and let myself out the front."

He rose and—did I imagine it?—made sure I was watching as he planted one very long kiss on my mother's mouth.

I turned to watch a neighbor across the alley taking out the garbage.

When I turned back, he had left, and Mom's face was bright, with pleasure rather than embarrassment, I thought.

"How do you like him?" she asked.

"He's not really my type, Mom, but then, he's your boyfriend."

She leaned toward me, and I smelled her jasmine. "What is your type, Jamie?"

I shrugged. "Don't know."

"But surely there are guys you have been interested in. What about that young man you dated at the beginning of junior year?"

Oh, yeah, him, the one I had fallen for big-time, never guessing that his one desire was to make varsity, and he figured that dating the coach's daughter would help.

"And the beginning of senior year," she added.

Burned once, shame on them, burned twice, shame on you. But I had thought this was a different situation; I had thought that Brett knew he had the starting tight-end position all wrapped up. Why either of those guys had thought Dad's decisions would be affected by who I dated, I had no idea.

"I have a lot of guy-friends," I told her. "You know, just friends," I explained, repeating the words I had come to hate. But that didn't deter my mother from a subject that held so much interest for her.

"Well, then, what's your dream guy like?"

"How would I know if I never met him?" I replied crossly.

"Easy. Imagine him," she said, with the reasoning of a writer. She wasn't going to give up.

"Maybe you've caught a glimpse of him," she suggested.

I sighed and searched for a description that would satisfy her. "He's the kind of guy, who, when you're feeling stupid and hurt and mad about something, something that's not even his fault, and when you're not looking and least expecting it, he gives you a rose."

My mother looked at me with surprise. "You *are* a romantic," she said.

Chapter 4

During dinner that night at Holy Frijoles on The Avenue, Mom talked about her new career in books and I about my career in high school sports, both of us avoiding the topic of guys. Later, I called Dad, as I had promised. I told him everything was great and didn't mention that Mom was seeing a Swedish trainer from her health club. Nor did I ask how Miss Matlock was doing with her cabin preparations. We stuck to the usual: the NBA playoffs and the Tigers.

Afterward, when I stuffed my sweaty clothes from the last two days in a laundry bag, I carefully removed the satin rose from my shirt strap.

It's pathetic, I told myself for the second time that day, when the most romantic gesture of your life was made by a guy in drag. Still, I was touched by his small, sweet gesture. I set the rose on top of my softball glove on a table next to my bed. At that moment, my mother walked in.

I was afraid she'd ask about the rose, but when she saw what I was wearing, she was too aghast to notice anything else. "Oh, baby," she said, "I need to get you to Victoria's Secret."

That must have been where she had bought her very sexy red silk nightie with its matching robe.

"I really like cotton," I said, fingering my Peyton Manning football shirt.

"The blue is nice, I suppose."

"The Colts will be glad to hear you like it," I told her, moving myself between her and the little table with the rose.

"We certainly have some shopping to do," she went on.

"It'll be fun," I lied. I enjoyed shopping, but not with my mother.

"Well, I thought I'd say good night and get my laptop." She closed the computer and picked it up. "I feel inspired tonight."

I didn't ask *by what?*

"Sleep as late as you like, baby. May I have a good-night kiss? Just tonight."

She rose up on her toes and I leaned down. "G'night, Mom."

I turned out the light right after that. The office had an air conditioner in one of the windows, but I switched on the ceiling fan and lay there listening to the night noises: people talking, people laughing, doors opening and closing, dogs barking, a car blaring music then roaring away, some softer music from someone's home. It was not nearly as peaceful as home in Michigan, but the city played its own kind of lullaby, and I was soon asleep.

When I woke up, the windows were closed and the sun was squeezing around the edges of the leopard valances and blinds. Mom must have come in and turned on the AC. I rolled over and looked at the clock. Eleven A.M.!

The moment I opened my bedroom door, I heard their laughter downstairs. Viktor was back. I guessed I'd do anything to avoid Sunday brunch with my mother's boyfriend. I slipped on a summer top and skirt, grabbed some money for something to eat, and told them I was going to church as I headed out the door. It left my mother speechless. If my father had heard, he would have been speechless as well, since I had fought him about going to church for the last three years. Actually, I was planning to find breakfast, but I came upon a church with a twelve o'clock mass and went in. The same old prayers were kind of comforting. In a summer where everything was changing in a bizarre way, maybe I needed one thing that didn't. Or maybe, with both my parents acting like teens, I had to be the adult. Whatever. I felt better, especially after I ate at Café Hon, and I walked home swinging my purse.

"Hi." It was a shy hello, from a great-looking guy sitting in front of Mom's house.

You *are way too young for her,* I felt like saying, then I realized he was sitting in front of his own place—the windows above the sidewalk matched up with his house, not ours. He must have been one of the Hopkins students.

"Hi, I'm Jamie."

He rose from his plastic chair and shook my hand.

If guys in college treated girls like this, I'm

going to enjoy it! I thought.

"I'm Ted. Ted Wu."

He was my height, Asian-American, with a perfect mix of features, magazine ad material.

"I'm spending the summer here with my mother," I explained.

"You're Rita's daughter? That must be something—to be Rita's daughter."

I wasn't sure what he meant by that, and decided I didn't want to know. I glanced in the direction of his radio, hearing phrases that sounded like a broadcast of a baseball game.

Ted reached out and politely turned down the volume.

"Don't do that. I love baseball," I said. "Is it the Orioles?"

"And Detroit Tigers."

"Oh, wow! I'm from Michigan. Who's pitching for the Tigers?"

"Bonderman. Want a chair?" he asked.

A few minutes later we were sitting side by side on folding chairs, our feet propped up on plastic crates, discussing the American league. We shared a passionate dislike for the Yankees, a love of any kind of football, and a preference for collegiate basketball over the NBA. Ted loved lacrosse and described the past season of Hopkins' Blue Jays.

I realized I was settling into another of my sports-buddy relationships, but I didn't care; I was so glad to have someone to hang out with.

"Want some iced tea? I grow mint in the backyard, if you like that in your tea."

"Cool."

While he fixed the tea, I went inside to change to a pair of shorts and a skinny-strapped shirt—might as well get a tan while I was sweating on the sidewalk. I made lots of noise as I walked down the narrow hall between the front door and stairway, so I wouldn't surprise Viktor and Mom.

"Just coming in to change my clothes," I called out.

I passed Viktor, who was in the middle bedroom, checking out a huge carton. It had a treadmill in it. I wondered why Mom, who was the sociable type and would prefer exercising at a gym, would purchase her own equipment. If anyone else had been in that room, I probably would have stopped to discuss training equipment, but I just waved as I went by.

"I see you've discovered stoop-sitting," said Viktor.

I backed up. "Stoop-sitting?"

"It's what they do here in Baltimore, sit on their front stoop, their little porches and steps, or even the sidewalk in between, and talk. I find it quaint."

Mr. Sophisticated World Traveler, I thought. "I find it fun."

"Especially with a college boy," he replied, breaking slowly into the smile that was too cosmetically perfect.

"Yeah, well, I really like being with people *my own age.*"

Continuing down the hall, I knew that I'd been obnoxious, but he really got on my nerves.

Mom was in the air-conditioned office-turned-bedroom. Her fingers fluttered up from the laptop keyboard in a short wave, then she went on typing as I changed clothes.

"I'm stoop-sitting," I told her, and headed back to the game.

By the seventh-inning stretch, Ted and I had moved to the backyard, which faced east and therefore supplied some shade close to the house. Ted had learned about Dad and Christine and Mom and Viktor. I had learned about his father, who was second-generation Chinese-American, and his mother, who was Canadian, and the Washington townhouse they called home—his dad was a congressman from California. It seemed as if Ted and I had been friends forever.

The game, which had been a pitchers' duel, took a sudden turn. The Orioles had bases loaded and two outs. "There's a swing and a long fly ball to center field," said the radio announcer.

"Yes, yes!" cried Ted, leaping from his chair.

"No, no!" I shouted, beating on the arm of mine.

"The center fielder is going back, reaching up—"

"No!" hollered Ted, waving his arms as if he could keep the Tiger from catching it.

"Ye—es!" I urged, my hands closing as if I were the center fielder feeling the ball land in my glove.

"He misses it! He lost it in the sun!"

"All-lll right!" exclaimed Ted.

"Aghhh!" I crumpled up on the ground,

feeling that a grand slam by the opposing team called for melodrama.

Ted laughed, and his gentle laughter was followed by laughter that was deeper. A tall guy wheeled through the back gate what was probably the most expensive bike I'd ever laid eyes on. Okay, so I noticed the bike first. I followed up with a much longer look at the guy, then dusted myself off and got back in my lawn chair, feeling stupid.

He gazed at me, his eyes bright with amusement . . . and interest? *Get a grip, Jamie.*

"Hey, Ted."

"Bring back a paper?" Ted asked.

"Two," the guy replied, wheeling his bike up the walk with one hand, swinging down his backpack with the other.

I was tempted to stand up as Ted had done for me, just to compare, but I remained seated, pretty sure he was several inches taller than me. He had dark hair and blue eyes, and long, tapered fingers, and was—what else can I say— overall gorgeous. I wondered why I had let my own small town convince me that there were no other kinds of guys in the world. Not that I thought a guy like him would be interested in me, but just his existence next door made me kind of hopeful and curious about what else was out there.

He set down his backpack, leaned his bike against his hip, and extended his hand. "I'm Andrew," he said, looking into my eyes.

"Hi."

After a moment he laughed. "And you are . . . ?"

"Oh. Jamie. Jamie Carvelli."

"Rita's daughter," Ted added.

"Really!"

Once again I wondered how others saw my mother and what that connection meant, but I had even less nerve to ask *him*. "Really."

"She's here for the summer, and in the fall, is going to be a Lady Terp. Got a basketball scholarship," Ted informed him.

"I'm sorry to hear you will be playing for the wrong team," Andrew said teasingly, "but I guess if *the* sports fan of the house can deal with it, I can."

He unzipped his knapsack. "*Post* or *Times*?" he asked Ted and me, taking out the Washington and New York newspapers. I was impressed.

"*Post*."

"Yeah, who wants to read about the Yankees?" I said.

Andrew laughed. "You're here for the whole summer? I don't know if I can take two sports addicts."

"Andrew is an arts guy," Ted said.

I could get into the arts, I thought.

"Any calls?" Andrew asked his housemate.

"Left them on the answering machine."

"Later," Andrew said, smiling at me, lifting his sleek titanium bike onto his shoulder and climbing the steps to the kitchen door.

"He doesn't have a steady girl," Ted told me when Andrew had disappeared.

I looked at him in surprise. Had my thoughts been written all over my face? If they had, I felt as if I had somehow betrayed Ted. "Did I ask?"

He smiled quietly. "No, but girls always do. So I thought you'd want to know."

I took a long drink of my iced tea. "Well, I think it's rude of those girls."

He shrugged. "Doesn't matter. I've got so much work when school's in session, I don't need distraction. Biochem is a tough major, and my parents expect nothing less than A's from me. Following sports is a lot more relaxing than dating."

"Tell me about it!"

We settled into an old-friend kind of ease with the game chatter between us, followed by the wrap-up of scores for the day. *Ted and Andrew versus Viktor,* I thought to myself. *Two to one in favor of a good summer.*

Chapter 5

By the next morning, the score had tipped the other way. First of all, Viktor spent the night. I holed up in my room early with the AC going full blast so I didn't have to hear their laughter, music, or anything else. Second of all, when I arrived at Stonegate's sports camp, I got a rude awakening.

The school itself, about two miles north of Mom's neighborhood, had impressive gates facing a wide, tree-lined avenue and a campus like a small college, with individual buildings for the lower, middle, and upper schools as well as a visual arts center, a performing arts center, a dining hall, two independent gymnasiums, multiple tennis courts, four baseball diamonds, and six soccer/lacrosse/hockey fields. Oh, yeah, and an Olympic-size indoor swimming pool.

That was not the rude awakening, of course; that was like walking into heaven. The shock came when I was assigned to the camp group I was going to spend the next five days with. Try to picture it: a six-foot college-bound girl surrounded by ninth graders who came up to her waist. All right, my elbow, and one or two to my shoulders, but I still looked like a crane that had gotten mixed up with the chickens.

"Excuse me," I said to the person who carried the clipboard with my name listed among the others. "I don't think I belong in this group."

The woman, who had thick yellow-and-gray hair and looked as if she had once carried a mean lacrosse stick, gazed up at me. "It said on your application that you don't have any game experience."

Thank you, Dad, I thought.

"Uh, well, we didn't have lacrosse teams where I lived, but I've played a lot of one-on-one, and practiced shooting."

"On a lacrosse field?"

"Against our garage," I replied, trying not to grit my teeth. "And whenever I could, I used the soccer goal at school."

"Most of the girls you are with, *in this group*, already have four years of competitive experience over you. Some of them have been playing since kindergarten."

I nodded, but wasn't going to give in. "I really would like a chance to work with the older girls."

"JOSH!" the woman hollered, blasting the ears of all of us who stood closer than the person she was summoning.

Across the field, the coach of the varsity girls looked up, then strode toward Ms. Mahler.

God, they grow them cute here! I thought. He was about my age, and not any taller than me—maybe an inch shorter—but he had incredibly broad shoulders and powerful arms and legs. I couldn't see his eyes beneath the shadow of his baseball cap, but I could see a strong jaw and a sweet mouth, and I could see that he was ignoring the titter of the girls on "my team," as they checked him out, keeping his focus on dear Ms. Mahler. His girls followed slowly behind him.

"Is there a problem?" I heard him ask.

Mahler pointed to her clipboard, then gestured toward me.

He glanced over his shoulder at me. Having been pegged as a "problem" for the first time in my athletic career, I gazed back at the two of them without blinking, folding my arms determinedly. I must have looked defiant, because he turned full face to me now, as if surprised.

"Never played a game in her life," Mahler said. "Fools around against the garage wall. Didn't play in a recreation league, didn't play at school, certainly didn't play elite, like some of our girls, but thinks she belongs with varsity. Give her a tryout."

"Two-v-two?" he asked.

"No, one-v-one, you and her. Let the others start their laps."

But the others weren't going anywhere — that was clear to me and should have been clear to her. Whispers spread throughout the group of varsity girls and giggles continued to come from "my" team, as Josh turned to look in my direction again.

"Mona, grab my stick," he said to one of his

players. "Got your mouthpiece?" he asked me.

I stuck it in with the attitude of a cowgirl strapping on her holster. Then I slipped on the protective eyewear. I knew what Ms. Mahler was doing. Seeing the little Blue Jay on the edge of this guy's shorts, I remembered the blurb in the camp brochure—he played for Hopkins. Mahler was going to make darn sure I got put in my place. If I failed, as she was sure I would, the rest of this week with her was going to be pure hell.

Well, little did she know. I'd much rather play against him than with girls, two-v-two. Dad had played for Maryland, another lacrosse powerhouse, and yeah, he was old, but I had spent my childhood learning rolls and dodges, trying to outwit him. My big drawback was that I had more experience with a guy's stick and had played guys' rules. In the last year I had been practicing with a girl's stick. My legs still knew what to do, but my cradle and shot weren't as good.

Josh plunked the ball in the head of my stick.

"You're using a guy's stick," he said.

"So are you," I shot back rashly. I was starting to feel cornered and angry, angry at Dad, Mom, Viktor, Ms. Mahler. . . .

He looked at me steadily. Close up, I could see his eyes were hazel—green, brown, dark gold—with the depth of the lake by our cabin.

"No, I am not," he said calmly. "When I'm here, I play girls' style with a girl's stick. How about you?"

I bit my lip.

"Mona, can she use your stick?" he called out.

"Don't bother. I brought another," I said.

I saw the flash in his eyes. "Oh, really? Then I suggest you get it."

I did, and he waited in his position as defender in a one-v-one exercise.

My initial moves were tentative. Josh played defense lightly, cutting me a break, which annoyed me. *If I just had my other stick,* I thought, as I made a lame feint to the left. But my father would never have put up with an excuse like that.

"Come on, girlfriend," someone yelled from the sidelines. "Strut your stuff."

It was the expression my best friend from Michigan used—strut your stuff. I began to move with more ease.

"Watch your cradle," said Josh. "Both hands. You're going to lose the ball with that stick. . . . Better, that's better."

"Thank you," I hissed, then I took off.

"Go get 'im, girlfriend!" my cheerleader hollered from the sidelines, and I did.

I dodged, I rolled, I faked, I dropped the ball and scooped it up again. I shot, I missed, I played the carom off the pipe—I had him sweating now—and I shot again, then cursed under my breath as I missed widely. We both raced, sticks banging at each other. I hit his stick away. Scooping the ball, I started to run again.

"Where are you going?" he called out, after a moment of watching me wander about the field.

Heck if I knew, I just needed to work off the edge of nervous energy, needed to buy time and think about adjustments, before trying a second time.

"Toward the goal, girlfriend, toward the goal," my cheerleader called.

We started again and now I was getting comfortable. Now, in my head, I was playing Dad. I was in the zone. I shifted to my left hand. Shot. Goal!

I fetched the ball and dropped it neatly into Josh's stick.

He didn't say anything, not an admiring "great shot, left-handed" nor a sneering "lucky shot, I could have played you tighter"—nothing. Oh, he was cool. Even while the others cheered, he was cool.

"Ready?" he said, as he shifted to offense.

"Don't I look ready?"

His reply was simply to cradle and run.

As he went through the motions, I was aware that he was testing me methodically, seeing how well I could backpedal, noting how fast I could change direction, working to find out if I was stronger defending on the left or the right. I was also aware that if he had been playing my father, he would have left Frank in the dust. There is something about top-notch athletes—their arms and legs are strung differently, move differently. Josh could have gone to the goal whenever he wanted, but he was having fun running me all over the field, seeing how I adjusted to his moves. He kept it up for what seemed like eternity, testing my endurance, and I started to get steamed. Instinct told me when he was finally going to make his move to the goal. And with instinct taking over, girls' rules went out the window. He made a quick feint to the inside, spun around, and—*whack*! Check—waist high and quite effective!

The ball flew sideways out of his netting, and bounced away from the goal harmlessly.

On the sideline his team erupted with cheers, then the younger girls imitated them and cheered, too.

"Girls' rules!" Josh shouted at me. His eyes blazed, turned almost amber. I knew I had ticked off a passionate competitor. And yeah, he was right, the check was illegal in girls' lacrosse.

Then he took a deep breath and got control of himself. He walked toward Mahler. "She plays like a guy."

Mahler nodded. "She's all yours, Josh."

I saw the expression on his face, a fleeting one, for he was too much of a pro to show what he felt, but I had caught that hundredth-of-a-second look, and it translated roughly as, *Don't do this to me*.

"Right," he said, then tossed his stick from one hand to the other and strode toward his team to pick up his clipboard. I slipped out my mouthpiece and followed him. My new campmates gathered around.

"Name?" he said, his eyes on his clipboard.

"Carvelli . . . Jamie."

"All right, Carvelli, you're warmed up so you can sit this out. Everyone else, a jog lap, then Michelle and Mona, you lead them into stretches."

"I do what everyone else on the team does," I informed him, which was obnoxious, given that I had just tried to sneak in a guy's stick. He gave me a look that said so. I gave a little shrug and joined the other girls in their jog.

Part of me was ashamed of the attitude I had adopted in the last fifteen minutes. I knew from listening to Dad over the years what a tough job coaching was and I'd always been respectful toward mine. Jogging with the pack,

I wished I had gotten off to a better start, wished it was already next week and I was working out at a Y somewhere.

"So who taught you to play?" asked the girl who was jogging to the right of me. I recognized the voice as belonging to my personal cheerleader.

"My dad."

"Obviously," said a blonde girl with a bouncing ponytail, who ran on my left.

"How come you never played on a team?" another girl called over her shoulder.

"Didn't have any. Lacrosse isn't big in my part of Michigan."

"What sport did you play?" my cheerleader asked.

"Basketball, Mona, obviously," answered the girl on my left.

"Maybe," replied Mona. "But I hate it when people assume stuff like that. If you're tall or you're black, they insist that you play basketball."

I glanced sideways at her. "Actually, I did play basketball."

"Me, too," she admitted—she was African American. "But I worship lacrosse. Fastest game on two feet."

"I'm glad we have an extra player," said a girl who had pulled up alongside the blonde on my left, and who was also blonde. We were a herd of blondish ponytails bouncing along, with Mona, two Chinese girls, and a redhead being the only exceptions among the sixteen players. "One more for a substitution when we scrimmage. Last year, Josh worked us till we were dead."

Apparently, Josh had the same goal this year. This wasn't some fluffy summer camp; he drilled us like he thought we were going pro, but he knew his stuff, and he knew how to teach.

After three hours, we were dismissed with the instruction to keep drinking water. I flopped on the grass, then a strong hand reached down and yanked me up. "Shade's over here," Mona said. I followed her to a spot beneath some leafy maples.

For a few moments we just sat and sucked on the straws of our water bottles.

"You're good. You'll pick it up fast," she said at last.

"Only if I can still walk tomorrow."

Mona laughed. "Having known you since nine A.M. today, I'm ready to predict that you'd play on your knees if you had to."

"I would."

She smiled. Mona was one of those rare people whose enthusiasm and friendliness made you forget her terrific looks. She could have been a statue in a museum, right there next to the Greek gods and athletes, with her powerful body, long neck, and high cheekbones. Her hair was pulled back sleek against her head, with thin braids wound at the nape. Monalisa Devine— even her name sounded Olympian to me.

We watched the other girls break into groups, with one large circle forming around the two blondes I'd talked to on the jog lap, Michelle and her sidekick, Brooke.

"It seems like a lot of the girls already know each other," I observed.

"A lot of us go to school here. That group, for instance," Mona said with a nod in Michelle's direction.

"You go to Stonegate?" I asked, then wished I hadn't sounded so surprised.

"I know, I don't quite fit in with the silky blonde ponytail crowd," she replied, then reached to pull on mine, as if to say, *no offense.* "It wasn't *my* first choice. My grandmother is big into education—she's a professor at Towson University. She raised me and wanted me to have the opportunities she had to fight for, even if it meant a lousy social life. Which it has. But the sports have been great, and if you want to learn, you definitely can in a place like this. Want a tour?"

"Yeah!"

The water had worked its magic, and I sprung up to collect my two sticks.

"We'll stash this stuff in my locker at the girls' gym," Monalisa said.

Halfway across the field we passed Ms. Mahler and Josh in an intense conversation. Ms. Mahler turned to look at us, which prompted Mona to smile and wave. Josh acted as if he didn't see us. When we had passed them Mona laughed to herself. "The big M, as we call her, is not at bad as you think. She's a fixture at

Stonegate and dates back from the time when people didn't take girls' sports seriously. So when you came in here carrying a guy's stick and assuming you could just jump right onto varsity, you set her off."

I nodded. "I can understand. I think I set both of them off."

"Oh, don't worry about Josh. He gets kind of strange and gruff when he's doing camp, probably because we're so close to his age and some of us knew him when he went to school here. He'll be a sophomore at Hopkins."

She turned to look over her shoulder, then waved her stick at him. I turned as well and Josh, who had been watching us, quickly showed us his back and continued his conversation with the big M.

"Hmm," Mona said. "Maybe you did set him off."

Chapter 6

"Monalisa Devine," my mother repeated. "What a wonderful name for a romantic heroine. I keep lists of names, you know."

I felt as if I were eight again, coming home from school, having a snack with my mother and talking over my day. It was a little weird, but nice. We sat behind the living room and stairway, in a small room with one window and the only AC unit on the first floor. Mom's house was like a train, with the living room, den, dining room, and kitchen lined up one behind the other, the house narrowing toward the rear to create an airway along one side.

"Are there other camps you can sign up for after this one?" Mom asked. "I'm doing all right financially, Jamie. I'd be glad to pay for another camp."

"There are all kinds of camps going on at Stonegate, guys' lacrosse in the afternoon, basketball next week, camps for underprivileged kids. It's wild. But I really should get a job, Mom."

"It's going to be hard to get one now, especially with you leaving for orientation in August."

"I know of a job," Viktor said, entering from the stairway hall. My head spun around. I wished he'd learn to make noise when he walked.

"They need a receptionist at the health club."

"Your health club?"

Can a guy smile coyly? Viktor did. "And your mother's."

"That's perfect, baby. And I'm sure they'd let you use the facilities as part of the benefits."

Oh, great, I thought, *I could work out right next to my mother and be instructed by her boyfriend.* I seized upon Mom's wise observation that most people didn't want to hire for a six- or seven-week period.

Viktor shrugged. "I won't tell them if you don't. You have to look out for yourself, Jamie. It isn't your job to worry about the problems of the manager and owner. That's the way the game goes."

"I'll think about it," I said, and took another chocolate cookie from the bag in front of me.

Perhaps I was being unfair. If Mona had said, "Hey, Jamie, you have to look out for yourself," maybe I would have heard it as a rallying call for a girl's right to do whatever. But coming from Viktor, I heard it as selfish and sneaky. I just could not cut the man a break.

"Where did you get those?" Viktor asked, as my mother reached for her third cookie.

"The bakery."

He looked at Mom as if she had just thrown back her fourth martini.

"Rita, I'm surprised at you," he said disapprovingly.

My mother gazed at the little white bag. "Jamie needs energy."

"Try one, they're good," I told him.

"Thank you. No," he answered coolly.

"Are you going to be downstairs for a

while?" I asked him. "Because I'd like to take a shower."

He understood that I expected full privacy on the second floor, at least for twenty minutes. "I'll stay down here."

As I rose to leave the room, I heard Mom say to him sweetly, "If you don't want this last cookie, darling, I'll take it," and I laughed to myself.

At dinner we made up for our sins from the bakery with some kind of veggie-and-tofu thing that Viktor made and that was, I had to admit, pretty good. After cleaning up, Mom and Viktor went for a walk down The Avenue. There was a building for lease, which he wanted her to see. I read the sports page and feature sections from cover to cover and wandered restlessly about the house. No baseball game was scheduled that night, and I felt a little shy about asking Ted to play catch with me. At last I grabbed my basketball and headed out back. I had noticed that several houses down, at the corner where our alley joined another alley at a right angle, there was an old hoop mounted on a board.

The basket had no net and the ball banged

loudly against the wooden backboard, rattling its rusty hoop. There were certain shots I couldn't take because one fence or another was in the way, but just the bounce-bounce-shoot rhythm soothed me. I had been shooting about fifteen minutes when Ted came out.

"Hey, Jamie."

"Hey, Ted, want to shoot around?"

"The thing is, I'm a great fan, but a lousy player."

"That doesn't matter to me. I'm just fooling around."

He opened the squeaky wire gate at the end of the yard and stood watching for a moment. I sensed he wanted to play, and passed the ball to him.

"I miss about ninety percent of the time," he said self-consciously.

"Perfect!" I replied. "You'll boost my ego, and believe me, I need it." I told him about my first day of lacrosse camp, the powerful Ms. Mahler, my face-off with Josh, and my struggle to learn the girls' game.

Ted listened quietly as we took turns shooting—he really wasn't bad—then said "Josh

Hammond? He's an incredible midfielder. You ought to see him play, Jamie. Next year he's going to be Hopkins's best all-around player. I predict it."

"Well, he's got a bit of an attitude," I said.

"He doesn't on the field. He's intense, but he's a team player. Actually, even off the field — he was in my lab last semester, and he didn't act like he thought he was cool or anything."

I shrugged. I didn't want to argue about it, especially since I may have been the one that caused the attitude. We continued to shoot.

"If you have any advice for me, Coach . . ." Ted said.

"Just a little. Relax your wrists."

The ball swished through the ring.

"Beauty!"

"Where do you think the foul line would be?" Ted asked.

I drew an imaginary line with my toe, and he positioned himself behind it.

"It's a tie game, three seconds left, and Wu is at the foul line," I said in an announcer's voice. "Ted has been the anchor of this year's team and is sporting a seventy percent free-throw aver-age."

Ted laughed at that, and I lined up along the imaginary lane.

"Will Wu's team go to the NCAA Semi-finals?"

Ted tossed up the ball. It came caroming off the rim.

"Rebound!" I screamed. "Carvelli has it. She dribbles, she clears, she turns, she shoots!"

Swish!

Ted's laughter was joined with someone else's, a quiet, resonant laugh. We both turned around.

"Hey, Andrew," Ted said. "Just get home?"

"About ten minutes ago."

He was smiling at me. "Hello, Jamie."

Sometimes, "hello" is a word intended to start a conversation. Sometimes it's a word used simply in passing. Once in a great while, if said slowly and with a slight tilt of the head, it expands into a long and tantalizing moment of just looking at each other. And did he ever know how to say it that way!

"Hi." My response was unimaginative and short. "Want to play?"

He laughed quietly. "One-on-one with Jamie in the moonlight."

A girl who had experience in romance rather than sports would have taken that bait and then offered her own, but I said, "You mean two-on-one."

He looked amused. "Two-on-one. You against Ted and me?"

"Okay."

He threw back his head and laughed.

"Don't laugh too hard," Ted informed his roommate. "You haven't seen what she can do."

"Oh, I've seen some. But actually, I came out to ask for help unloading my Jeep."

"Did you get the bookcases?" Ted asked.

"Yep, I'm parked out front."

"I can unload," I offered.

"You can admire," Andrew replied, and opened the gate for us.

I tossed my basketball into my mother's yard and followed them through the house. I was told to hold the door, and did so, but thought it was dumb given all the boxes that needed to be brought in.

"Are you building a library?" I asked.

"He *has* a library; he's building shelves for it," Ted replied. "Andrew's an English major. And a writer."

"No kidding! My mom's a writer." The moment I spoke those words, I wanted to suck them back into my mouth.

"She is?" Andrew looked at me with surprise. "She is?" he said, turning to Ted as if wondering why Ted had never mentioned this. "What does she write?"

I hesitated. "Books."

He laughed.

"Popular fiction," I said, thinking it sounded better than steamy romances. "That's why she's home so much."

"Oh. I assumed she was just a divorcée living off her husband's income."

"Mom supports herself. She always has."

Hearing the edge in my voice, he threw up his hands in surrender. "I never really talked to her, Jamie, so I didn't know. I've just seen her, and that blond guy, going in and out."

I didn't identify "that blond guy" for him.

Ted had sat down on the floor and opened one of the boxes. "These bookcases are going to be terrific," he said.

"Where's your toolbox?" Andrew asked.

"In my room."

As Andrew headed upstairs, Ted motioned to me. I sat next to him on the rug. "I know your mom writes romances," Ted said in a low voice. "That's cool. But I never thought to mention it to Andrew. He's a poet and into writing a lot of profound stuff, if you know what I mean. When he and Rita meet outside, they look at each other as if they're from different planets."

"They are," I said.

Ted nodded. "I like your mother. Maybe because you love sports and we're the same age, but when I started listening to spring baseball, she and I sort of connected. She talks a lot about you, you know. I knew all about you before you came."

I blushed, ashamed of myself for not admitting my mother's line of work when, apparently, she bragged about me.

Hearing footsteps on the upstairs landing,

Ted began pulling the heavy boards from the IKEA boxes.

"God, I'm glad you're organized," Andrew said, as he set down the toolbox and dropped to his knees. "If you're given a choice, Jamie, choose a science major for a roommate."

"But maybe she likes stepping around books and fighting her way through snowdrifts of papers," Ted teased him.

"Ted said you're a poet," I prompted.

Andrew, who was pulling instructions from one of the boxes, paused to look at me. He hadn't shaved for at least a day and his beard was rough. His blue eyes sparkled with mischief. "That's right. I scribble images."

"I like to read what other people write," I said, not wanting to be too pushy and ask directly to read his work.

He smiled. "You're a sweet girl."

What did that mean? Was it a pat on the head?

"Want to hang out and help us put these together?" Ted asked me.

I glanced toward the toolbox. I could handle a screwdriver and hammer, and I'd much rather spend the evening at Ted and Andrew's house than my mother's. But this was just the kind of togetherness that got me into being thought of as another "guy."

"Thanks, but I have some things of my own to take care of," I lied. "Let me know when I can come back and admire."

Chapter 7

"*L*adies, I expect you to be on time," Josh lectured us the next morning. "I expect you to be well-rested, and well-fed, *Amanda*—" she shoved the last bit of bagel in her mouth and licked the cream cheese off her fingers, "properly equipped, and *on time*."

Yes, Mother Superior, I thought. I must have muttered without realizing it, because several girls turned toward me.

"Jamie, do you have something to say?"

"No . . ." This time I definitely muttered and somebody giggled. Josh and I were off to another great start.

"Okay, the three who just arrived, do your jog lap and stretches. Everyone else, line up for partner passing, ten strong hand, ten opposite hand, and so on till I tell you to stop."

Michelle and Brooke, who had strolled in late wearing short pajama bottoms (Michelle's had sleeping kittens on it), began their lap with Amanda. Monalisa asked me to be her partner, which was nice of her given that, if I didn't keep my focus, I tended to drive the ball into the ground with my girl's stick.

"Do anything interesting last night?" Mona asked, as we got into a rhythm of back and forth.

"Played basketball in the alley, watched guys lug boxes into a house, and fell in love."

"Whoa!" Mona exclaimed.

"Just kidding," I said quickly, "about the last part, I mean."

"Well, maybe, you fell in *like*?" Mona suggested.

My lousy pass skittered past her. "Maybe."

After fifteen minutes of the passing drill, Josh called us together and went over the basics of shooting. We were split into two groups, with a goalie assigned to each group, and lined up along the eight-meter fans for a "rapid-fire" drill, practicing high, mid, and low shots into the goal, each girl having her own ball, giving the goalies a workout. At nine forty we got our first break.

"So tell me about him," said Mona, as every-one gathered around to drop balls in the bag Josh was holding.

"His name is Andrew. He's great-looking," I began, "and he's taller than me."

Everybody's eyes flicked to the top of my head, as if they had just pulled out imaginary yardsticks.

"Six feet," I said automatically, "I am six feet exactly."

"How tall are you, Josh?" Brooke asked.

"Five eleven."

Mona knew better than to ask anything more about "him" in front of the others.

"And?" Michelle prompted, her eyes fixed on me.

"And what?"

"Well, it can't be just his height that makes this guy so great, although I can see how that would be an issue for you."

Everyone was listening, including Josh.

I gazed down on her dark roots—she stood maybe five-five. "I was talking to Mona, okay?"

"I was just being interested," she replied.

Giving a grade-school toss of her ponytail, she walked away.

Josh wore a poker face—coaching girls, he probably had seen this kind of thing before. Brooke followed Michelle, but the others, even the members of their Stonegate School clique, looked uncertain for a moment, as if they were hoping for more details. I guess all girls are interested in hearing about somebody else's love life. The problem was, I didn't have one. And I couldn't believe Andrew would want to go out with me—and I really didn't want Michelle to observe once again that she could see how this was "an issue" for me.

Monalisa gave me a light push in the oppo-site direction. "Sorry," she said, "I got you into that."

A heavyset girl named Amber, who played goalie and had just proven herself to be a human octopus with remarkable reflexes, followed us, as did three blonde ponytails and a braid. It would have been snobby not to include the others, so we dropped down on the grass and talked about summer stuff, vacations, part-time jobs, et cetera. Mona and the girl with the braid,

Brittany, had jobs that I would like, working at camps for the summer. Mona was coaching several sessions at Stonegate, including basketball camp with middle-school girls.

We came back to play three-v-three at each end of the field, three girls versus three plus a goalie, then moved on to four-v-four, playing just one end of the field, so that Josh could stop us in midaction and teach. He rotated us in and out of positions and expected us to be totally involved whether we were playing or watching. Being desperate to learn the sport and prove myself good at it, I was very attentive, but others received laserlike glances from him when they started fooling around. He didn't seem to get that this was a *summer* camp.

When I played, he yelled at me constantly, but I didn't mind. "Watch your stick, Jamie, your stick. You're going to lose the ball!" And just as he'd say that, I'd lose it, because I had held my stick too straight up, like a guy's. My old stick had felt like an extension of my hand, the same way my baseball glove felt like a mere improvement on my palm and fingers. The girl's stick felt like a tool that I couldn't control without constantly thinking about it, an effort that distracted me from the game action.

Then suddenly, the stick began to feel right, began to feel like mine. I raced after the ball as it flew past the goal, scooped it, fed Brittany from behind the goal—nice shot, blocked by Amber—Kate played the carom, passed it to me, I cradled, dodged, spun, faked out Michelle (oh, the joy!), and prepared to sidearm a shot past Brooke.

Plunk. The ball fell out of my stick. Just like that, *plunk.*

I was furious. I slammed my stick into the ground and had a wild four-year-old impulse to jump up and down on it, to break the stupid stick into a thousand pieces, which would have been tough, given it was metal. Then I came to my senses. I peeked around at the others, who were staring at me, and felt the color creeping into my cheeks. "Excuse me," I said in a tiny voice.

"It's okay," Josh replied. "It's frustrating, especially when you're used to succeeding." His voice was surprisingly gentle.

I caught the arched-eyebrow exchange between Michelle and Brooke, and ignored it. They were used to succeeding, too, and probably resented an amateur struggling to learn their game. I didn't know if Amber caught their look. She lifted her mask and said encouragingly, "Try it again, Jamie. I want the fun of blocking your shot!"

"Okay. I will!"

We played on. I was good at defense, partly because my height gave me tremendous range with my stick. On offense, I settled for more conservative moves, concentrating on getting the ball to my teammates when they were in a good position to shoot. But then the opportunity came again. Mona had rotated into the scrimmage and slipped me the ball, knowing from either watching me play or perhaps instinct, that I would have taken the ball and run if I'd held a guy's stick.

"You go, girl!" Josh shouted at me, and I did.

I dodged Michelle and ripped the shot into the net.

"Goal!" cried Mona.

Amber grinned at me. "I let you have that one."

"Yeah, yeah," I replied, grinning back.

"Nice one, Jamie," Josh said. I basked in the

restrained but—from him—meaningful praise. I could still hear his enthusiastic "You go, girl!" ringing in my ears.

He pulled me out then. I knew the coaching strategy: Let the player end her day on a positive note.

A few minutes later, Michelle and Brooke joined me on the sideline.

"Looks like the coach has a favorite," Michelle remarked to Brooke, loud enough for everyone along the sideline to hear. Out of the corner of my eye, I saw the others lean toward her, listening. I kept my eyes on Mona, trying to learn from her, mentally holding the stick like she did and studying her footwork.

"I bet he wouldn't mind giving Jamie a little extra time when we're finished today," Michelle went on.

"Some one-v-one, some personal instruction on *technique*," Brooke replied.

They're just having fun with me, I thought. *Let it pass.*

Then Kelly, the redhead, said, "Last year, Jamie, several of us tried seducing Josh."

"Why?"

The sideline broke out in laughter, which was quieted by a glance from Josh. "Ladies, stay with the game. You're here to learn."

"Why?" the girl next to Kelly repeated after me. "Are you blind, Jamie? On a scale of one to ten, he's a twelve."

"He *is* an inch shorter than her," Michelle pointed out sweetly.

"Still, I would think she'd like the challenge," Brooke said, doing that annoying thing of talking *about* someone rather than *to* them, then scooting closer to me on the grass. "Wouldn't you?"

"He's not my kind of challenge," I told her.

"Oh, guys like Josh are easy," said a girl named Melanie. From various conversations, I had gathered that she was transferring to Stonegate and had been working hard to get accepted into Michelle's group. She had the required blonde ponytail, but her most noticeable feature was an astounding set of boobs. Given this attribute, most guys probably *were* easy for her—at least, getting them to look at her would be easy.

"Guys like Josh—" she gave a knowing shrug—"they look tough, cool, like they could have anyone and they're really not interested in you. But when they fall in love, they go straight off the deep end. I could bring Josh to his knees."

"I bet," I muttered. You would think that I had learned earlier not to mutter.

"Take her on," Michelle urged.

"Do it!" Brooke said. "How much do you want to bet?"

"I was talking to myself," I explained quickly, but they already knew that.

Melanie glanced from princess number one to princess number two of the clique that she so badly wanted admittance to. She turned to me. "Backing out?"

"We have only three days left," I pointed out. "You'd have to work awfully fast."

She smiled at me. "I always do."

"Of course, we should set the rules and conditions with that in mind," Michelle said.

"Maybe if you can just get him to ask you out," Brooke suggested.

"Good luck on that," Kelly responded. "Knowing how Josh acted last summer, I think Melanie should win if *she* asks, and he agrees to go out with her."

"That sounds fair," Melanie said.

"But what if he's only being polite?" I argued.

"Not Josh," said Kelly, as if she knew from experience.

"Twenty dollars," Melanie proposed.

"Twenty bucks?!" I exclaimed.

"What I want to know," Michelle said, "is whether Jamie can try to interfere. Can she try to get him to go out with her first?"

"No," I replied firmly.

"Great idea!" Brooke said.

"Nooooo."

"Okay, ten dollars," Melanie proposed, "just because I feel like I'm taking candy from a baby."

Who was the baby, Josh or me, I wondered.

A shrill whistle split our ears.

"Ladies," Josh hollered—he had been trying to get our attention—"are you going to join us for the wrap-up, or shall we carry on into the afternoon?"

We scrambled to our feet and joined the players on the field to hear an evaluation of our progress and Josh's plan for tomorrow. Then we did the traditional "raise your stick and give a shout."

Little did Josh know that a second game plan was being drawn up.

Chapter 8

"Do you have time for lunch?" Mona asked me.

"Sure." Stonegate had a dining hall rather than a cafeteria, and it was stocked like a gourmet delicatessen.

"I can't believe how fast you're progressing," Mona said, as we walked toward the building, she swinging her stick, me cradling an imaginary ball. "Even Josh was impressed."

I grimaced at the mention of him. How could I have gotten entangled in such a stupid bet?

Mona misinterpreted my expression. "Why don't you like Josh?"

"What do you mean? I like him. I respect him. He knows his stuff."

She stopped and studied me, her dark, curly-lashed eyes probing my face. I was beginning to feel really uneasy about the bet and looked away.

"I guess I have a soft spot for him," Mona said, as we continued walking. "He was raised by his grandmother, like me. And if you think parents who are twenty-five years older than you are tough, try parents who are fifty."

"What happened to his mom and dad?" I asked.

"I don't know. Josh is a private person, and personal info has to be dragged out of him. But I know he and his grandmother don't have much money. They live in an old house in Waverly and he drives an ancient Toyota. He came to Stonegate in middle school on one of those scholarships for bright underprivileged kids. By the time he finished here, he not only had aced all his subjects, but learned lacrosse and got a scholarship to Hopkins. The other kids here, including myself, have our way paid by our families. Everything Josh has, he's earned."

I was silent until we put in our lunch orders. Maybe that's why he acted as if our little summer camp was an Olympic training ground. "He doesn't take opportunities for granted," I said.

"He doesn't take anything for granted."

We took our sandwiches out to a picnic bench next to the dining hall.

"Tell me about your family," Mona said. "I know your Dad's a coach, but you're with your mom now, right? Because you're going to Maryland in the fall?"

"Not exactly." I told her about Dad and Christine, then Mom and Victor. She had finished her lunch and I hadn't started mine.

"Girlfriend, that is so cool," Mona said, "having a mother who's a romance writer!"

"Cool, Mona, is having a grandmother who is a history professor. I bet your grandmother doesn't leave Post-its around with juicy plot ideas and hot images, the kind you don't want to read when other people are there. "

She laughed out loud. "No, our Post-its say things like 'Drop off dry cleaning,' and 'Dept. Meeting, Thurs @ 4.' But the world needs both profs and steamy writers," she added philosophically. "At least, *I* need both."

"I guess I do, too," I admitted.

"So, let's go ogle some guys." She glanced

at her watch. "Their lacrosse camp starts in ten minutes. They play in the heat of the day and start stripping in no time."

"But guys wear equipment."

"I mean on the sidelines, hon," she said, slipping into Bawlmerese, "which is where we'll be."

Mona and I watched the guys' camp for an hour and a half, analyzing everything from great shoulders and tight buns to effective footwork. "Ah," Mona said, stretching back on the grass, then rolling on her side, so she could continue to observe. "This is how spectator sports are meant to be experienced."

She saw my eyes drifting to the field behind us, where Josh worked with JV-level players, guys too young for us. "I know," she said, "he's good with us, but he's better with them. I don't know why he's so uptight this year, except of course, that we're close to his age, and several of the girls tried to come on to him last year."

I felt the color creeping into my face.

"It was embarrassing."

"Yeah."

Mona sat up. "You were thinking of doing

that?" she asked, misinterpreting my guilty blush.

"No, no."

"It's okay, just wait till after camp," she advised.

"But I'm not," I insisted.

An hour later, as I let myself into the house, I decided to call off the bet and pay off Melanie, even pay her the twenty bucks if I had to.

I found my mother typing on her laptop, sitting close to the air conditioner in the room behind the living room, dressed in a stretchy pink tank top with a tiny border of lace, pink shorts, and jeweled sandals. I was pretty sure Mona's grandmother didn't wear that kind of outfit. Post-its were stuck at odd angles on the wall next to her.

She raised one hand from the keyboard. "Hi, baby."

"How did you know it was me and not Viktor?" I asked, since she hadn't looked up.

She typed another line, then turned to me. "I can hear you walk."

"Mom, you should work in your office. I

don't need the room except to sleep. I feel like I'm pushing you out of your own spot."

She dismissed the concern with a freshly painted set of nails. "When no one else is home, I find I can concentrate here," she replied. "And I'm starting to grow attached to my pets."

"Your pets?"

She pointed to the two pigeons that were sitting outside the window on the AC unit. "Brad and Andrea, the hero and heroine of *Heat Lightning*," she added, referring to her current book.

The birds had found a comfortable roost in the narrow strip of daylight that slipped between the opposing walls of the back of our rowhouse and the house next door.

"How do you tell males and female pigeons apart?"

"I have no idea," she admitted. "They could be Brad and Andrew. But they coo so sweetly, and I like their company. Writing can be lonely."

I hadn't thought about that, what it was like to go from being a middle school teacher with kids and other teachers around you every day to writing full-time. Maybe that explained Viktor. I looked down at the droppings outside the window. "You need a cat, Mom."

"Viktor doesn't like them. He says they slink around."

Like he does, I thought, but I wouldn't hurt her feelings by saying it.

"I'm on a roll, Jamie, so I'm going to keep writing. A new batch of cookies is hidden in the empty box of Kashi. Oh, and there was something pushed through the mail slot for you. It's on the table in the living room."

I grabbed three cookies and headed to the front room, curious. A sheet of newspaper had been folded several times to make a rectangle, with my name written across it in a felt tip pen. I unfolded the paper and read the fluid backhand script:

> *Jamie,*
> *This looks like a fabulous film.*
> *Would you come see it with me? Wed*
> *evening, 8 o'clock viewing.*
> *Andrew*

I read it twice more. *He's asking me out*, I thought. *This gorgeous guy is actually asking me out.* And he wasn't saying, "Hey, Jamie, want to hang with the guys at Sammy's? Bring the chips." He was issuing an invitation for a real date.

I read the printed background of his note, which was a review of the movie. French, with subtitles, the film's name translated as *The Dream of the Boar.* Okay, large bristly pigs who spoke French were not my first choice of movie subject, and I doubted I'd get all the layers of meaning that the reviewer enjoyed, but it was a date with Andrew. And I could always tape the baseball game.

I hurried upstairs to write a quick response on a piece of my mother's nicer paper. Then I placed the movie review under my pink satin rose.

Andrew called that evening to say he'd drive and that we should leave about seven fifteen the next day. I could hear soft, jazzy music playing in the background. Mona called as I was ripping open boxes and throwing clothes on the leopard bedspread, trying to figure out what to wear to the movies.

"Hi. What are you doing?" Mona asked.

"Wishing I had done some laundry before packing my clothes in Michigan."

She laughed, then I told her about my date with Andrew and my various choices in clothes — that is, once I washed them.

"My advice is to wear what you most enjoy wearing. If you're comfortable, you'll shine, Jamie."

"That makes too much sense," I replied.

"Listen," Mona went on, "I called with some awesome news. Hannah, the girl who was doing basketball camp with me, is sick. Well, that's not awesome, but here's what is. The big M needs a replacement for next week. Interested?"

"Are you kidding? I'd love it. But Ms. Mahler will never hire me."

"I already talked to her about it, and she wants you to come in early tomorrow to fill out an application."

"You must have given quite a recommendation."

"Actually, she nabbed Josh, who was on

a water break with the JV guys, and said she wanted an honest evaluation, a character reference, as she put it, since, obviously, we know you have the basketball skills to teach middle school girls. He said he didn't know anything about your organizational ability, but in terms of your passion for athletics, he thought you'd be terrific. . . . Are you there?"

I was surprised by the flush of pleasure I felt, knowing Josh had recommended me.

"Jamie?"

"I'm here."

"There are other camps, like the afternoon one for city kids who don't have a place to play. Hannah was supposed to do that, too. Are you interested?" she asked.

"Oh, yeah!" I said. "Oh, yeah!"

Chapter 9

Wednesday morning, as I walked across the grass to Stonegate's PE offices, I was feeling high as the June sun. In just a few days, my doomed summer had taken surprising and happy turns. I had a chance at a job for next week, maybe longer. I had a date with Andrew tonight. I was getting better at lacrosse. That morning, I'd even enjoyed Viktor's "power breakfast."

Ms. Mahler was waiting for me in her office. She didn't seem any friendlier than when she had told Josh, "She's all yours." But she didn't seem unfriendly, either, and as I handed her my application, she said, "Congratulations on being a Maryland Terp." I thanked her and left.

Outside the birds were twittering away. Mona came galloping across the field to me and we laughed and walked together toward the girls' practice field. Then I saw Melanie.

To be fair, if she had bound her boobs with an Ace bandage and duct tape, they still would have been . . . well, prominent. But the shirt she wore today was outrageous. Mona spotted her talking to Josh the same time I did, and she groaned in response. "Here we go again."

We were ten minutes early, and only Amber and Kate, both of whom were dropped off by somebody on their way to work, had arrived. We joined them on the bench.

"I've got cleavage like that," Amber said. "Unfortunately, I also have a waist and hips about three times the size of hers."

"*I've* got cleavage like that, too," Kate boasted, and we looked at her questioningly, because she was definitely on the wiry side. "I just like to keep my ass covered."

Mona folded her hands as if she were praying. "God, help me resist zinging a chest-high pass."

I would have laughed if I hadn't felt partially responsible. I told myself that the boobs were there before the bet. But she definitely had herself on display now. I could never figure out how girls could be so obvious and guys could be such suckers, but I had seen it over and over at my high school, and I knew that the strategy worked.

Several other girls arrived, and comments continued to fly.

"Are breast steroids illegal?" asked Brittany.

Michelle and Brooke arrived three minutes before nine, completing the group, and Josh congratulated us on our promptness. Since he and I were nearly the same height, and Melanie was about five seven, I knew that when he looked down at her, he had the same great perspective of the cleavage.

She bounced through our jog lap and stretches, attended by Michelle and Brooke. Just before we started our drills, I got her alone for a moment.

"Melanie, we've got to talk."

"Not now, everyone's lining up."

"This won't take long. The bet's off."

She laughed a tinkling kind of laugh. "I don't think so."

"I know so."

"But I've barely started," she said. "And I'm enjoying it." She wriggled her shoulders. "It makes sweating worthwhile."

"Cut it out," I told her. "It's not fair to Josh."

"Oh, my," she cooed. "You sound worried—worried about losing."

"That's not the point," I snapped. "I'm paying you the ten bucks now, and I want you to—"

"Ladies," Josh called with strained patience. "Would you like to be part of this?"

Melanie and I turned to see that everyone was in position for the drill. She trotted off like a perky cheerleader and I joined the group at the opposite end.

"What were you saying to her?" Mona asked me when the drill was done and we were setting up for the next one.

I couldn't admit to her that I had made the bet, so I avoided the question, asking back, "Do you have an extra T-shirt in your locker?"

She crinkled up her brow. "For Melanie?"

"Is there someone else who needs it?"

"Don't be offended, Jamie, but you're naive. Nothing stops girls like that, not T-shirts, not suits of armor."

I sighed.

"Don't worry," Mona said calmly. "Josh can be very cool when he has to be."

"According to Melanie, she can bring cool guys like him to their knees. The cooler they are, the harder they fall."

"When did she say that?"

"Yesterday. You were scrimmaging." It was the perfect opportunity to admit to the bet, but I couldn't.

Mona shook her head, then we lined up for the ladder drill, an exercise with a ladder made of two pieces of rope and plastic bars, designed to improve your footwork. I had done it frequently enough and should have been good at it.

"Focus, Carvelli," Josh barked at me as I continued to screw up.

During our first water break, without giving us a chance to kick back and talk, Josh launched into a discussion of defensive strategy. I figured that he could see the group was distracted and was attempting to keep us on track. But by the time we had sweated ourselves up to the second break, it occurred to me that he might have had another reason to talk to us as a group: the wish to avoid a one-v-one conversation with Miss Cleavage.

It was hotter than it had been the first two days, with a forecast for temperatures in the mid-nineties. We flopped on the grass beneath the trees and drained our water bottles—all of us except Melanie. She had questions for Josh and stood just about beneath his nose while she asked them, forcing him to look down. We watched and drank and mopped our foreheads.

"Poor little thing," Amber said, pulling on the neckline of her extra-large T-shirt. "She's just standing there trickling water. Somebody should wring her out."

"We could take up a collection and get her a sweatband," Kelly suggested. "Two of them, one for each boob."

The other girls laughed, including Michelle and Brooke, who weren't above snickering at the girl who obviously wanted to join their clique.

I didn't laugh, and Monalisa studied me for a moment. "Girl, you had better drink a lot of water," she said quietly, "because it's coming out your ears as steam."

Before we began to scrimmage, five-v-five,

Josh warned us about managing the heat. "Each of you is responsible for monitoring yourself," he reminded us. "The temperature is climbing, and the humidity is high. You have to let me know when you're feeling the heat."

"I'm feeling the heat," Melanie said, and several girls laughed.

"We haven't begun to play yet," Josh replied, then he called out the names of the first and second teams, handing out pinnies to the first team. They pulled on the red nylon vests that were used to identify them as a "team" during practice. Melanie was assigned a pinny.

"I guess he noticed," said someone.

"He's a guy, isn't he?"

Mona was assigned to Melanie's team, playing midfielder, which meant she'd be passing the ball to Melanie, who was a forward. "God, help me resist," she said, winking at me. When I grimaced, she gave me a poke with her stick. "Lighten up, Jamie."

During the twenty-minute period, Josh rotated us in and out, doing his best to keep us from overheating. Finally, Melanie and I ended up on the sidelines at the same time.

"We've got to talk," I said, as we stood side by side.

The other girls on the sideline edged closer. "The bet is off, Melanie. It was a stupid bet and it's off."

"I'd say it's on," Melanie replied. "At least, I'm on, and I'm going to win this thing."

"Okay. You've won. You're the winner—you can bring any guy to his knees. It's over," I reached in my shorts pocket for the money I'd put in there that morning.

"The question is whether I can bring *Josh* to his knees," Melanie observed.

"You've convinced me," I said, pressing the ten-dollar bill, damp with sweat, into her hand.

She handed it back. "I haven't even started."

"Bet's over," I said, placing the money in her palm and closing her fingers around it.

"Ow!" she squealed. "That's my shooting hand."

But I hadn't hurt her, as was evident by the way she shoved the cash back into my pocket.

"Don't you understand?" I said, my voice beginning to rise. "Don't you get it?" I pulled out a second ten. "Here, twenty bucks, that's what you wanted."

"Don't *you* get it?" she replied. "You can't change the rules halfway through. You can't back out." She dropped the two bills, letting them flutter down to my feet. "They're sticky," she said.

I snatched up the money. "Good. Because this money is going to stick." I pushed it down the front of her bra. It stuck all right.

That's when I noticed the unusual silence on the field around us. Without looking, I knew the scrimmage had stopped. When I glanced sideways, I saw the other players staring at us, frozen like statues in some kind of sports hall of fame. Mona's mouth was open. Josh's mouth was closed, but he was speechless, at least for the moment. I turned back to Melanie. Two little tens peeked up from her cleavage. She laughed.

"Melanie, do walk-laps, five of them, this field," Josh said sternly. "Jamie, same thing, next field. Find your cooler heads, ladies, or I'll ask you to leave."

So I went into exile. And frankly, I wanted to stay there. I had graduated from high school, why should I still have to deal with girls like Melanie? It wasn't my idea to attend this stupid camp. It was my father's way of making himself look like a good guy.

Oh, I was doing a great job of walking and feeling sorry for myself. I nearly walked right into Ms. Mahler, who had just sent her team on break. She raised an eyebrow at me, wondering what I was doing on her field.

"I'm, uh, finding my cooler head," I said, using Josh's words.

"Good," she replied, with a brisk nod, and went on with her business. I realized I had better get on with mine.

When I got closer to the varsity field, I called to Josh, "Can I jog the laps to get them over with and get back in the game?"

He nodded.

I ran them, and after another water break, he did put me back in, with Melanie on my team.

I didn't have to worry about the other girls' comments or even a question or two from Mona. Everyone was acting like Olympic hopefuls now, making their best efforts to focus on practice.

Josh called us together at five minutes to

twelve, gave us a rundown of tomorrow, and reminded us to "Drink water, drink water, drink water." Then we lifted our sticks and gave a shout.

A few minutes later, when I opened my backpack to get out another bottle of water, I saw the twenty dollars lying on my towel. I took a good long drink, zipped up the pack, and heaved it onto my shoulder. When I stood up, my legs felt tired and rubbery.

"You okay?" Mona asked.

"Yup."

"Jamie."

I turned in Josh's direction.

"May I see you for a minute?"

"Sure." I grabbed my stick and headed toward him, noticing that Mona stayed discreetly behind. Most everyone else had cleared out.

He didn't speak right away. His sunglasses were up on his head and I found myself wishing he'd wear them so I wouldn't have to meet his eyes.

"Look," he said, "I'm not interested in what you and Melanie were fighting about."

Oh, but you should be, I thought.

"But I am really surprised. And disappointed."

My heart drooped a little. He was an athlete—he had to know that disappointing your coach felt worse than making him angry.

"I didn't think you'd let yourself get sucked into that group, Jamie."

I hadn't thought so, either. Still, I got defensive. "But you don't really know me, do you?" I replied.

I saw him blink, then he looked away for a moment. "No, I guess I don't. But I know this much," he said, his eyes narrowing into certainty, "you could be a great player if you applied yourself. You have the talent. It's all a matter of desire and discipline."

I shrugged, then gazed down at my feet.

"All right. See you tomorrow." He picked up the bag of balls and headed in the direction of the PE offices.

"Are you sorry you recommended me to Ms. Mahler?" I called after him. It was dumb, but I had to know.

He turned back and studied me for a

moment, his head tilted to one side. I couldn't stand the tension. "There's probably time to change it," I baited him.

"Don't test me, Jamie," he said, and walked away.

Chapter 10

"You sure know how to create some excitement," Mona observed as we walked to our cars. She had wanted to grab lunch at the dining hall, but I had a raging headache.

"Go home, turn up the AC, take a long bubble bath, and sip some raspberry tea," she advised. "You've got to be in shape for Andrew tonight."

"Oh, God, Andrew," I said. "I forgot."

"Pull yourself together, girlfriend! And if you think you'll need a sub, let me know. Otherwise, I want all the details tomorrow — on the date and on what exactly happened today between you and Melanie."

"Right," I said, throwing a towel onto the seat of my broiling car, driving off before I even opened the windows. I was that desperate to get away from Stonegate's fields.

As soon as I got home, I gathered up a huge basket of laundry, with underwear and everything else that I might need for tonight, and hauled it down to the washer in the basement. Returning to the kitchen, I found a coded note from my mother:

> *Jamie,*
> *I'll be back by 4:45.*
> *There's plenty of Kashi.*
> *Look by your bed — I found a box of*
> *your old books.*

I ate a yogurt then dove into the Kashi box, which was filled with cookies. When my wash was done, I flipped it over to the dryer and headed up to my room. Taking Mona's advice, I shut the door and clicked the AC on high. *Ahh!* The headache was already disappearing. Next to my daybed sat a dusty-looking carton. I pulled books from it, picture books with covers and pages that had been turned over and over, and occasionally colored on: *The Berenstain*

Bears Go Out for the Team, *The Berenstain Bears and the Female Fullback*, *Cinderella*, *Snow White*, *Rapunzel*, *Sleeping Beauty*—my favorite old books. The illustrations for the fairy tales were beautiful. Making myself comfortable on the leopard spread, I began to read. I didn't realize how tired I was.

At four twenty I discovered I had fallen under the spell of the bad fairy, and one look in the bathroom mirror told me it wasn't Sleeping Beauty who had just awakened. I peeled off my sweat-encrusted clothes and took a shower, using one of my mother's fancy shampoos. I came out smelling like jasmine, and by the time I smoothed on some of the loveliest lotion I'd ever felt, I was a virtual flower garden. I pulled out a drawer in the vanity and searched through her bottles of nail polish. There were a zillion pinks, lavenders, and peaches. I chose peach because it seemed summery and looked good with the tan I was starting to get. I had just finished my toes and one hand when the doorbell rang. I glanced at the small clock Mom kept in the bathroom. Four forty-five. *Mom will get it,* I thought.

I waved my left hand around, trying to get it to dry, and the doorbell rang again. *She must have locked herself out,* I thought. My robe was down in the dryer, so I grabbed Mom's from the bathroom hook, giggling a little as I ran downstairs. It was that slinky red thing with a plunging neckline and a ridiculous ruffle that, because of our difference in heights, ran short around my thighs.

"Coming," I called to her, then pulled open the door.

For a moment, he and I stood there just staring at each other. I squinted into the sunlight, thinking I was seeing things; he peered into the darkness of the house, obviously thinking the same thing.

"Josh! What are you doing here?"

"Jamie?" He sounded incredulous.

Well, who else? I thought, then I remembered what I was wearing. Oh, my God!

His eyes moved slowly from my loose, damp hair to my shoulders, took a meandering trip down to my legs, then made a daylong journey to my painted toes. It was my imagination, it had to be my imagination, but I felt heat under my skin every inch of the way.

"What are you doing here?" I repeated.

"I was going to ask you the same thing," he said.

"I live here."

"With Carolyn Velli?" He reached into his pocket. "Maybe I have the wrong address."

That's when I noticed the books in his hands.

"She's my mother, which is who I thought *you* were when the doorbell rang. Carolyn Velli . . . Car-velli? Get it? Her real name is Rita."

"O-oh."

There was a moment of silence, as if we both needed time to recover our breath from the shock we had just sustained.

"Somehow, I didn't think you'd be the type to read her books," I said at last.

At that he smiled. "My grandmother is a huge fan, and I was supposed to get these books signed for her at HonFest, but I forgot. So I went to your mother's website and e-mailed her. She said I could bring them by today at four forty-five."

I nodded. It was all starting to make sense.

"Well then, you may as well come in."

He stepped inside and surveyed the room with undisguised curiosity, taking in the artificial flowers that draped the windows, the piles of purple and pink pillows, and the fringed lilac shades, his eyes finally coming to rest on my heart-framed face resting among the zillion candles on our fake fireplace.

"Just for the record," I said, "my clothes are in the dryer, so I grabbed my mother's robe to answer the door."

He turned to me, smiled, and said nothing, which sent the blood rushing to my cheeks.

"Sit down," I ordered. "She'll be here soon. I'm getting my clothes."

Retreating to the basement, I pulled my wrinkled clothes from the dryer and changed into shorts and a T-shirt right there, unwilling to pass by Josh once more in that red silky thing. As I carried the laundry basket upstairs, I heard my mother unlocking the front door.

"I'm so sorry I'm late," I heard her gush. Her hair, which she had pinned up because of the heat, was coming down in curly gold strands, making her look flustered and pretty. She dropped a pile of grocery bags in the entrance hall.

Josh leaped to his feet. "Can I help you with those?"

"That would be wonderful," she said.

"Hi, Mom."

"Hi, baby. I have more groceries in the car."

"I'll get them," Josh told her.

My mother batted her eyes at him. "I'd be so appreciative."

"No problem."

Since they seemed to be determined to charm each other, I let him be chivalrous and simply picked up the bags in the hall and carried them into the kitchen.

"I wish all young men were so thoughtful," my mother said, following me, her big blue alligator purse swinging from her shoulder. "I'm so glad you were here to let him in."

"You could have warned me he was coming," I replied.

We began pulling items out of the bag — more cookies, pasta, and bacon, food that had to be on Viktor's sin list.

"There wasn't any reason to. Signing books is business, not a social occasion, although it is a very pleasant part of my business," she admitted.

"Mom, he's Josh. You know, as in Josh, my coach."

"Your coach?" Her mascara-thick eyelashes flicked with surprise. "You mean your lacrosse coach? Why, it never occurred to me! He was so delightful in his e-mail, it never crossed my mind he could be the Josh you said was—" She stopped, for Josh had come in with the second load of groceries.

He smiled at her. "Go on."

"Too serious and authoritarian."

You'd think that, being a writer, she could have found another way to put it.

Josh glanced at me and smirked a little. "Well, for the record," he said, echoing my words from a few minutes before, "your daughter doesn't come off quite the same as she does at practice."

I blushed and my mother looked at me questioningly.

"Excuse me, while I put my laundry away," I said.

As I folded, I listened to the sound from the dining room, the murmur of their voices, punctuated by laughter. It occurred to me that having spent nine hours of practice with Josh, I had never heard him laugh.

I finished putting away my laundry and could have painted the rest of my nails, but I felt jittery. For some reason, his presence in our house disturbed me—seeing this other part of his personality made me feel edgy. I thought she said this wasn't supposed to be a social visit.

Finally I went downstairs. As soon as Josh saw me, he stood up.

"Ah," sighed my mother, "it's so rare nowadays for a man to stand when a woman enters a room."

"I think he was leaving, Mom," I replied.

"Leaving? Not yet. Perhaps you would like to stay for dinner," she invited.

Dinner? Had she forgotten my date? She was the one who had suggested this morning that we eat early so I'd have time to "pretty up."

"I'm sorry. My grandmother probably has something prepared," Josh replied politely.

"Another night, then," Mom said, and

turned to me. "I'll get started on ours. Why don't you two go play some hoop, bunny?"

I looked at her as if she had lost it.

"That's what her father used to say," my mother explained to Josh, then made her voice deep in imitation of him. "Hey, want to go play some hoop, bunny?"

Josh rubbed his hand over his mouth in a feeble attempt to hide his laughter, his eyes crinkling up.

"Our little baby—well, she wasn't so little, not even when she was born—hopped around like a bunny since she was fourteen months."

He laughed. "Do you have a basketball net here?" he asked me.

"There's a hoop about three houses down, at the end of the alley, but that's all it is, a rusty rim and a rickety backboard."

His eyes were bright. "Want to?"

Maybe it was the light in his eyes, a playfulness I hadn't seen before. Maybe it was that basketball was the one way I could count on getting back my dignity. I glanced at the clock. There was still plenty of time to "pretty up." "All right."

I ran upstairs to grab my shoes and ball, then led the way out back. Ted had just returned from his lab job and was sitting on the back porch, sipping some of his mint tea.

"Want to play?" I asked him.

"It's ninety-four degrees," he replied. "I'm going to hang out here and resuscitate you if you need it. Then he turned to Josh. "Hi."

"Hi. It's Ted, right? You were in my Chem lab last semester."

"Yes." Ted looked pleased that Josh remembered him.

"We had a terrible TA," Josh explained to me. "Whenever we had a question, we asked Ted."

My baseball buddy smiled self-consciously and seemed to be at a loss for words.

"He knows just as much about sports," I said, then continued down the walk to the back alley, realizing Ted would be way too shy to play in front of Josh.

"The fences make it kind of a challenge," I told Josh, "especially in that corner." I pointed to where our alley met the other one. "Don't impale yourself on a picket."

"Darn. That's just where I take my three-point shot. The one I always make. "

"Un-hunh."

Actually, he was good at shooting, having the hand-eye coordination that is the gift of an excellent athlete.

"So let me see you jump, bunny," he said after several minutes of quiet shooting.

I flashed him a look and he grinned back at me.

"No one calls me that but my parents."

He laughed and tossed me the ball. "Can you dunk it, bunny?"

"No one calls me that!"

"Yeah, yeah. Let's see what you can do, rabbit."

I pivoted on the exact spot where I was standing, twenty-five feet from the basket, and plunked it in. Which wasn't easy, since I had made a point of shooting flat-footed.

"That's great," he said, "as long as there isn't a defender in sight." After scooping up the ball, he walked it back to me and stood face-to-face. "C'mon," he urged, his voice low and per-suasive.

I faked to the left and went right, faking him out but good, then stubbornly shot flat-footed again.

"Funny thing," I said, smiling slyly, "there wasn't a defender in sight."

"Yeah, well, we'll see about that. One-on-one," he proposed.

"It's kind of hot for that."

"Excuses," he replied, then added, "We can even use a *guy's* basketball."

There is only one kind of basketball, of course, but I took the bait, as he knew I would. Monday's one-on-one was his game; this one-on-one was mine.

We both played hard, driving, faking, spinning, shooting, crashing "the boards" for the rebound, slamming into each other. Every jump was a competition in timing as well as height. Our arms got tangled up, and our feet—once I sent him sprawling. Shoulder against shoulder, hip against hip. Lots of sweat. I was shooting through a screen of tumbling hair.

"Time out," I said, catching hold of my wild hair, trying to smooth it and weave it into a braid.

Josh dribbled the ball, waiting for me. My fingers were halfway down the braid when I heard the bouncing stop. I finished the braid, twisted it around itself and pulled the end through in a kind of knot. When I glanced up, Josh was watching me.

A soft golden light shone in his hazel eyes. *It's the evening sun,* I told myself. It's the slant of the light when the sun is in the west. Still, it drew me, the way the warmth of the sun does.

I pulled my eyes away. "Ready."

We started playing again. I drove, I faked, I leaped, I shot, just like before. I crashed the boards with him, just like before. I played my toughest defense and blocked a shot, just like before. But the game felt different. I was playing the exact same way I played the guys at home, but I was so . . . so *aware* of him—aware of the edge of his shoe against mine, aware of the slightest brush of his arm. In the last four years of pickup games, I had slammed against a lot of hard and heaving chests; why was I suddenly noticing his?

It's the romances, I thought. It's those stupid books! Romance writers were always talking about hard chests and tingling touches. I had to stop reading them.

We played on—me, getting way too serious about a back-alley game, because I was trying to keep my focus on the sport, and Josh just laughing. Every time he laughed, I felt as well as heard it, as if his laughter were rumbling inside me.

I played harder, if that were possible. When the ball caromed wide off the rim, I flew after it. One moment I saw the ball floating in the air, almost within reach, the next, I saw a row of sharp pickets coming at me. Just before I skewered myself on the fence, an arm reached around my waist and yanked me back. We spun together and slammed against the wooden boards.

"You trying to kill yourself?" Josh asked.

"Just rebounding."

With him standing behind me, holding me tightly against him, I was aware of how broad his shoulders were, how he could enfold me like a protective cape.

"Sometimes," I said, "all I see is the ball."

He laughed quietly, his mouth close to my

ear. "I know how that is."

Did he also know what weird things my senses were doing? His quick breath was making a strand of my hair dance against my cheek, and my whole body tingled.

Then someone had a coughing fit. Ted was coughing loud enough to scare off the most determined city pigeons. I suddenly saw the basketball again, lying among a row of tomato plants. At that moment, Josh let go. As he reached for the gate latch to enter the garden, I heard another gate squeak and I turned around.

"Hello, Jamie."

"Andrew. Hi."

"I wanted to let you know what time we should leave tonight."

I looked at him, confused. I thought we had already settled the time.

"There's going to be a crowd, so I think we ought to take off about seven fifteen."

That's what he had said last night.

Josh, ball tucked under one arm, sweating an ocean, stood several feet behind me, as if he didn't want to interrupt.

"Okay?"

"Sure. I'm halfway ready," I replied, holding up the hand with the painted nails. Three were chipped now, my hair was mess, and I needed another shower. "See you then."

"I'd better go," Josh said, as I turned to him. He waved to Ted, who waved back, and we walked silently to the house. Once inside he snatched up his books from the kitchen table. "Thanks, Mrs. Carvelli. Gran's going to be really excited."

"Rita. Call me Rita. Are you leaving?"

"Not without water," I interjected.

He shook his head. "Thanks, I'm fine."

"Drink water, drink water, drink water," I reminded him, using the words he always used at the end of practice.

It was like breaking a spell.

"Right," he replied in that crisp tone of voice he used at camp, accepting the bottle I thrust in his hand.

"See you tomorrow," I said.

"Nine o'clock," my coach replied firmly, and left.

Chapter 11

Of course, the bristly pigs didn't speak French. It was a group of medieval guys running around in *The Hunt for the Wild Boar* who created the need for subtitles. I was grateful for the dialogue printed at the bottom of the screen: It gave me something to read when "the pursuit of life in all its wondrous brutality," which Andrew told me was the film's theme, got gory. I really don't like gore, but I would not have admitted that to Andrew any more than I would have to my guy friends at home, who loved blood—although they preferred it in English.

Just being at the Charles Theater, an arts cinema, and studying the people in the ticket line was a cultural experience. Andrew ran into several friends, one girl with a streak of Goth,

another with some serious glasses and braini-
ness that were awesome when coupled with her
very short skirt and tight knit top. She had come
with her British friend, Fiona, who was an art
major and considered *herself* an important work.
Earlier that evening, when I had met Andrew on
the sidewalk between our houses, dressed in my
camisole and capris, with my fingernails and
toenails painted and hair falling just right for
once, I felt incredibly good about the way I
looked. After meeting the girls he considered
friends, I felt as boring as a Sears ad.

The guys he knew were just as interesting—
two with beards, one with long shining hair
bound at the back of his neck with a piece of
leather. He had great, rugged-looking features
and could have worn a tutu without making
people snicker. All of Andrew's friends talked
film, dropping names of movies and directors I
had never heard of. I was relieved, but also a
little disappointed, when Andrew turned down
two different invitations to join them after the
movie.

We went alone to a sushi place. Normally, a
day of sports camp and some pickup basketball

would have left me hungry for a hamburger topped with bacon and cheese, but after watching guys slaughter a boar, a restaurant that served orange, pink, and white platters of fish was a good choice. I was fascinated by the ease with which Andrew did everything, from talking artsy, to guiding the car through city traffic, to asking the waiter about new items on the menu in a way that suggested he had spent half his life in Japan.

"So," he said, after our order had been taken, and warm, moist hand cloths had been brought to our table. "You haven't said a word about the film. Did you enjoy it?"

"It was . . . it was interesting."

One side of his mouth drew up. "But not your type of flick."

"I think I'd have to see several more movies like it before I could say that," I replied. "It was new to me, that's all. I didn't know any of the movies your friends were talking about." *I may as well admit it,* I thought; I certainly couldn't fake it. "How do you know whether you're really going to enjoy something before you've tried it a few times?"

Andrew smiled and touched my hand lightly. "Oh, sometimes you just know." The way his hand grazed mine made me think he wasn't referring to the movie.

Having decided earlier that I must stop reading romances, I now thought I had to read more, so I could figure out how to respond to gestures and words that seemed like part of a romantic movie.

Andrew sat back in his chair. "I applaud your openness to trying something new, Jamie." He sounded a little like a teacher, but his eyes were warm. "Essentially, the film was a dream vision, a medieval form in which the protagonist is dealing with an internal struggle, falls asleep and has a vision, often one of a hunt, in which he enters a forest—the green wood that we see later in Shakespeare's comedies—and pursues the beast. He acts in a way that resolves his internal conflict, which allows him to reenter the civilized world."

"Oh."

"I want to try writing a contemporary dream vision. My poems are rich in imagery, as dream visions are, and I'm exceptionally good at narrative. I've always been drawn to the more profound questions of life."

The platter of sushi was placed between us.

"So I believe I'm a natural for the genre." He lifted a piece of tuna with his chopsticks. "In fact, I think I can take it to a whole new level. I consider myself an innovator. Aren't you hungry, Jamie?"

"Would it embarrass you if I asked for a fork?"

He raised his hand as if he had experience in summoning waiters in restaurants across two continents. "Would you bring the lady a fork?" he asked the man, then went on. "I'm feeling rather constricted by traditional forms, and find free verse uninspiring. I want to explore new ways of expressing myself. I have so much to share with others."

"Writing is hard work," I said, contributing the one thing I knew about the topic. "I've seen it with my mother."

"Your mother?"

"She's a writer," I reminded him.

"Not quite the same type as I," he replied.

"Well, she's published three books, but

you're still in college. You have to give your-self time."

He frowned, and for a moment I thought he looked insulted. "That's not exactly what I meant. Rita is more of an entertainer."

In other words, she wasn't profound. But it seemed to me that she also had a lot to share with others. "She entertains with words that are printed on a page. Why wouldn't that be writing?" I asked, unexpectedly defensive of Mom. Of course, I would have died before let-ting him see the working notes she had scrib-bled on her Post-its.

I sat back as the waiter placed a fork by my hand.

Andrew leaned toward me. "Let's talk about you, not your mom," he said with a smile. "Tell me about yourself, Jamie Carvelli. What is Jamie short for?"

"Jamie."

His blue eyes twinkled, as if he were amused. "Do you have a middle name?"

"Rita."

I had the fleeting thought that I should have made up a different one. "How about you?" I asked. "What's your middle name?"

"Hunterton. It's an old family name."

"Andrew Hunterton Wilcox. Cool."

"You know, I loved watching you play basketball today," he said. "It was like watching a ballet."

"A ballet?"

He smiled.

"I—I never thought of it that way."

"Mmm." He looked off in the distance, as if he were seeing a vision of me and Josh in the back alley. "The give and take between you and your opponent, your steps matched and countered by his, your wonderful grace and strength."

I blinked, trying to replace my sweaty vision with Andrew's.

"The sum of grace and strength," he went on, his voice musical, as if he were reciting poetry. "What better definition is there of beauty?"

I blushed. Was he saying I was beautiful?

"Grace and strength—and vulnerability," he added, one finger gently lifting my chin so I would look at him. I gazed back, words failing me again.

He laughed quietly and let go.

"When I was watching you play," he went on, "a million lines went through my head."

"Like what?" I asked, curious, and yes, fishing for a compliment.

"*How can we know the dancer from the dance?*"

"Wow."

"I'm quoting Yeats, of course."

"Wow all the same."

He laughed. "You're charming."

It was an old-fashioned description, but a big improvement over all those guys in high school slapping me on the back and saying, "You're the best, Jamie"—especially when spoken by a guy resting his chin on his hand, looking at me as if he'd be content to do so all night.

Andrew quoted a lot of poets that night as we talked on about movies, music, and a little about sports. I learned that his family was from Connecticut, that his dad was an exec at an investment firm, and his older brother a lawyer, which he didn't seem to think much of. "Lawyers abuse words," he said. "They trap with words. Words are precious things meant to create, to imagine, to dream with."

Speaking of dreaming, this was like one, and I wanted to stay, but I was struggling to keep my eyes open.

"I should take you home," Andrew said, and I nodded meekly.

On the way home, I fell sound asleep. One moment I was riding in his Jeep, wind blowing my hair, enjoying the romance of the city at night. The next moment, the custom leather seat, wider than my own shoulders, seemed to enfold me like a protective cape. I relaxed against it and felt Josh laughing softly, whispering in my ear, "I know how that is."

I became aware of a face close to mine and a hand playing with a strand of my hair. "Sleeping Beauty," his voice said, oh, so seductively. "Sleeping Beauty, shall I awaken you with a kiss?"

I opened my eyes and was momentarily confused when Andrew's lips touched mine.

"I had a wonderful time, Jamie. Thank you," he said.

"Me too . . . Me too."

Inside my head, the various scenes from the long day were colliding, making me dizzy. I was so slow getting out of the Jeep, he gallantly opened the door, and helped me slide down from the seat, then waited for me while I struggled to unlock the front door.

"Thank you, Andrew. G'night."

When I had shut the front door, I leaned back against it, eyes closed for a moment, summoning the energy to climb the steps and set my alarm for tomorrow's camp.

"Have a good time?"

My eyes flew open. Now I was awake. Viktor had entered from the room behind the living room.

"Yes," I said.

"Is he as sexy as he is rich?" Viktor asked.

I stared at him. "Why would you even think I'd share something like that with you?"

"I'm just being friendly," Viktor replied with a small shrug. "And I thought you might make an effort to be friendly, too. After all, I *am* rather important to your mother."

"I know that."

In the dim light provided by the small lamp left on for me, Viktor sized me up. "You resent me. You never expected to run home to Mommy and find her with a lover."

I nodded. I certainly couldn't deny it.

"Think about it from my point of view," he said. "I never expected my lover to suddenly have a kid again. She didn't tell me you were coming until the day you arrived."

I bit my lip. I had been so caught up in my own situation, I hadn't thought about it from anyone else's perspective. I had put Mom in a bad position. "I guess we both have to get used to each other," I said. "And it might take a while."

"In the meantime," he told me, "don't encourage Rita to stop by the bakery."

"You've been into the Kashi," I said.

"The refrigerator is now full of junk," he went on. "It took me four months to get her into barely reasonable shape. Don't sabotage my efforts."

I prickled. Barely reasonable shape? She was fifty, what did he expect? Aloud I said, "What Mom buys and what Mom eats is her choice, not mine."

"You know what I —"

"And by the way, it's not your choice, either."

He met my eyes straight on. "Like I said, you resent me."

"I resent anyone who tries to control another person," I told him, and headed for the stairs.

Chapter 12

Thursday morning I arrived at camp three minutes late.

"Carvelli," Josh said to me, with a flick of his head toward the other girls who were doing their warm-up jog, "an extra lap."

I guess it was naive to think he'd say something like, "Good morning, Jamie. It was fun yesterday."

Without a word, I started my laps then joined the others in their stretches.

"Hey, sleepyhead," Mona greeted me.

"Hey, Jamie," a chorus of others chimed in.

"Must have been some date last night," Mona teased.

"I was three stupid minutes late!"

Amber straightened up and grinned at me.

"Look at your T-shirt, Jamie."

Glancing down, I saw that it was on backward. No wonder it was uncomfortable. Instinctively, I checked for the label in my shorts, and everyone laughed.

"Keep with it, ladies," Josh called from the bench, where he stood, one foot on the metal, and studying his clipboard.

"He's on a mission today," Brittany said.

"He's on a mission every day," replied Kate.

I did my stretches but my shirt kept pulling under my armpits, driving me crazy. "Mona, hold down the edge of my shirt, okay?"

She did, and I drew in my arms, pulling my hands through the sleeves just as Josh looked over. With my arms on the inside, I turned inside the shirt, like I was inside a barrel, then stuck my hands through the proper holes. Josh rubbed his forehead and looked away.

"If you wore stretchy tanks like Melanie," Kate whispered to me, "it wouldn't matter which is the front and which is the back."

Today's sexy tank top was tropical blue, but it had the same effect as yesterday's. Apparently, word had gotten around campus: The school's maintenance crew was taking its morning break at our field, and I was pretty sure it wasn't because they were interested in lacrosse drills.

We started with a shuttle drill, passing on the move, then a drill for scooping up ground balls. Josh took us to the other end of the field, and I figured it was because picking up ground balls requires a lot of leaning over. By that time, maintenance had to get back to work, but a crew of painters had arrived for a coffee break and simply shifted their positions to accommodate the drill.

Josh looked like he had a migraine. I saw that Mona was gritting her teeth.

"That girl has no shame!" Mona said to me at a water break.

"Mona, we had a bet," I blurted out.

She stared at me. "I'm sorry?"

"Melanie and I had a bet," I said.

"Tell me you didn't."

I held the cold water bottle to my forehead.

"Girlfriend," Mona demanded. "Speak!"

"I bet her that she couldn't seduce Josh— but listen, listen first—listen why I did."

"There can be no good reason why!"

I had the feeling I was looking into the eyes of Mona's grandmother.

"They said I was his favorite and tried to get *me* to seduce him, and I said he wasn't my type, and then Melanie said guys like him were easy, and that she could bring him to his knees, and then I muttered something stupid like yeah, I bet, and then they said, how much?"

"And your answer was *nothing*," Mona responded, her eyes flashing. "At least it should have been."

"I told them I was just talking to myself, but they kept at it, Michelle and Brooke. And Melanie wanted to be in cool with them, so she wouldn't let it go. I gave in. I was an idiot and gave in."

"And yesterday, on the sidelines, you tried to end the bet." Mona's voice was a little less fierce. "That's what that was all about."

"Yeah, but she wouldn't let me. I offered her twice the amount of money, but she's got something to prove. There's nothing I can do about it."

"You can tell Josh."

"What?"

"Listen to me, Jamie. Stuff like this can get a coach in big trouble—you know that, your dad's a coach."

"Yeah, but Josh is innocent. I mean, it's not like he's taken the bait . . . so far."

"If it comes to *he said, she said*, it doesn't matter. You owe it to him to warn him, to give him the heads-up."

He's going to hate me forever, I thought.

"Don't you get it?" she went on. "Josh needs this job, he needs it for the rest of the summer. Maybe you don't have to work, and I know I don't, except that my grandmother would have my hide if I didn't, but he and his gran really do need him to work. Are you going to chance screwing that up?"

"Is after practice soon enough?"

She nodded. "For him, yes. For her, I don't know. I may knock her unconscious before the next break," Mona said, with a glance in Melanie's direction. Melanie was talking to Josh, drinking from her water bottle and throwing back her head as she did. I sighed. Nice view.

I spent the rest of practice dreading twelve o'clock. Josh barked at me twice, then seemed to decide it was best to leave me alone. Finally we lifted our sticks in the air and gave a shout, then I hung out with Mona, waiting for my chance to talk to Josh after the others left.

He had gathered his clipboard, gym bag, and bag of balls, when I called out to him. "Josh, can I talk to you?"

He turned and for a moment I thought he was going to say no.

"All right."

Meanwhile, Mona was cutting across the field, fast.

"Where are you going?" I cried.

"I'll meet you at the dining hall, if you want."

What I wanted was for her to stay with me for moral support, but she was moving quickly.

I walked over to the bench, keeping a good five feet between Josh and me. "It's about yesterday, and today, and actually, the day before, and I guess tomorrow, too," I began awkwardly.

"Well, that's every day but Monday," he observed.

"Yeah."

He set down his gear, realizing this wasn't

going to come out easily.

"It's about Melanie and me."

"Jamie, I don't think it's wise for me to get involved with whatever's going on between two people I'm coaching. If we were a team, and I thought it was affecting the way we worked as a team, then I would have to be involved, but since we are not—"

"And you," I said, "it's about you, too."

He got a wary look in his eyes.

"I made a bet with her. I bet that she couldn't seduce you."

Josh's mouth opened, then closed, then opened again.

"Some of the girls said they tried to last year."

He just stared at me.

"And they said, like, I was your favorite and that maybe you'd . . ." my voice trailed off as I saw him take a deep breath and let it out slowly. "Well, anyway, they told me I should try to—to get a date or something. And I told them that you weren't my kind of challenge."

"I see," he said.

"I'm not finished. So then Melanie said that

guys like you were easy. You look cool, you look tough, but when you fall, you fall like a ton of bricks. Well, those weren't her exact words—*cool*, *tough*, and *easy* were, but not the ton of bricks. What she said was that guys like you, when you fall for a girl, go 'straight off the deep end.'"

"I see."

"She said she could bring you to your knees."

"And you were happy to encourage her." The accusation was like a rope he snapped in the air.

"No, no, it wasn't like that. I didn't want to encourage her, I was just a coward about saying no, about telling her right then that it was a stupid idea. I tried to end the bet the next day, yesterday, when you saw us fighting on the sideline. I tried paying her off, with twice as much, twenty dollars," I added, hoping he'd realize how sincere my effort was.

"An impressive amount," he noted dryly.

"Try to understand."

"I'm trying."

Now I was getting mad, getting defensive.

"Are you telling me you've never made a stupid bet in your life? Are you so cool and in charge you've never wanted to take back words the moment you said them?"

He blinked and looked away.

"I'm sorry, Josh. I really am."

He didn't say anything.

"I guess it's too soon to ask for forgiveness."

He turned to me, his eyes dark with anger. "Jamie, do you have any idea what kind of trouble I could get into if Melanie succeeded, or if someone simply *perceived* her as succeeding?"

"Yes. Mona made it pretty clear. And I should have thought about it even before that, since my dad's a coach. I'm sorry, Josh."

He stared out toward the goal.

"I don't know what else to say."

He picked up his things, but didn't move farther.

"Um, do you want me to come tomorrow, or would you prefer me to call in sick?"

He silently beat his lacrosse stick against his leg, as if a long argument were going on inside him. "See you nine o'clock . . . sharp," he added, but his voice had lost its energy.

"Thanks."

I left him standing at the edge of the field, still staring at the goal. I had one more task, which could best be done while he wasn't around. I headed for the PE offices.

When I arrived, Ms. Mahler had just dropped off her equipment from the JV session and was leaving for lunch.

"Can I talk to you?" I asked.

"One fifteen," she told me.

"No, please, I need to now. Before I lose my nerve."

We went into her office and I told her the whole ridiculous story, every detail I could think of, determined to make sure that Josh was in the clear. She listened without interruption, without asking a single question or voicing an opinion. When I was finished and had lapsed into silence, she said, "Sometimes I think I've been doing this job too long." That was it, nothing else.

I left, and if I'd had a tail, it would have been between my legs.

"So did you get the job?" Ted asked as we sat on the sidewalk in front of our houses

Thursday evening, listening to the game.

"After what I've done, it'll take a miracle."

"What did you do?" Ted asked.

I told him about the miserable mess. He listened and thought about it, while the Orioles loaded the bases then struck out.

"You were trapped, Jamie," he said, as a car commercial came on. "I don't think what you did was so awful, and you did try to fix it. Once Josh thinks through the situation, he won't hold it against you. He's too nice a guy, and too level-headed."

"Mona said the same thing today at lunch. But I think I bring out some other side of him. I think that the Josh who most people know and the Josh I know are different."

"Which Josh was the one you played yesterday?" Ted asked.

I glanced over at him. We sat like guys do, side by side gazing straight ahead while we talked, but I looked at him now, wondering whether he had noticed that strange magic spell I had felt. "What do you mean?"

He smile and shrugged. "Just wondering."

I shifted in my plastic chair. "I think the

Orioles need a better setup man for their closer."

Because Ted was a guy, he let me get away with changing the subject. Eventually, I was able to push aside all thoughts about Josh and relax enough to enjoy the sultry evening. There were no bright stars, like at my home in Michigan, but the streetlamps winked on and I could see the storefronts glowing at the corners of Chestnut and The Avenue. Summer in the city had its own beauty and romance—if you were with the right person.

The Orioles loaded the bases again. Just as they scored the first run, Andrew drove up in his Jeep. He climbed out looking tired and scruffy, his jeans and shirt covered with dirt. I thought he looked cuter than ever—maybe he was the kind of guy who cleaned up too well; maybe he should let himself go a little more.

Ted greeted him. "Looks like a long day in the land of lawn-and-gardens."

"I did some private contracting after hours," Andrew replied. "They pay well in Roland Park, but they know how to work you. Hi, Jamie."

"Hi, Andrew. Have a seat." I offered him mine, moving from my chair to the front steps.

"Thanks, no, I need a shower. I think I need a blast with a fire hose. But I'm glad I ran into you. Are you free tomorrow night?"

Would saying yes on such short notice make me seem too eager? Maybe, but I wasn't good at playing hard to get. "Yes."

"Have you been to the harbor?"

"No. I'd love to see it."

He smiled. "Then you shall. We'll take a water taxi tour. Dinner at eight?"

It sounded like a movie—I think it *was* a movie.

"Okay."

"We'll leave here seven fifteen-ish," he said. "See you then."

I moved back into my chair, and Ted and I went on with baseball talk. For the first time that week, I wished that Ted was Mona, and we could discuss clothes for tomorrow night. She'd given me her phone number, but it seemed rude to get up and call her. *There will be time to talk before camp,* I thought. I appreciated the second chance Josh was giving me, and I planned to be there, ready to play, long before nine o'clock . . . sharp.

Chapter 13

Maybe it was out of respect for Josh, or maybe it was a kind of sentimental thing about the last day of camp, but all of us arrived early on Friday. Josh was clearly the coach again, not anything like the guy I had left staring at the goal, much less the one I had played basketball with. The others would never have guessed I had told him about the bet. Everything was cool.

Of course, Melanie came in her best tank top, one with stripes that accented contours that needed no accents. We had another audience of maintenance workers, and this time a crew from the phone company joined them. Josh gave us girls plenty of encouragement. I knew this strategy, too: hard on the team at the beginning of the "season," and positive toward the end.

At one point, when Ms. Mahler's players were on break, she came to our field to watch. I was in the scrimmage then and played the best I had all week.

"You've outdone yourself, girlfriend," Mona said, giving me a high five.

I had to—I had to prove to the big M that I was capable of learning, and I had to make Josh proud.

At fifteen minutes to twelve, he called us together, sat us on the bench, and gave us an evaluation, telling each of us what our strength was and what we needed to work on next. Then we stood up, raised our sticks, and gave a shout. It was over—that fast.

As people gathered their things and exchanged e-mail addresses, Josh turned to me. "Jamie, Ms. Mahler would like to see you in her office."

Uh-oh, I thought. She hadn't said anything yesterday, and now I was going to hear it. "Okay," I replied aloud, then glanced at Mona.

"I'll wait for you at the dining hall," she said quietly.

"Thanks. Order me a grilled chicken, and don't wait for me to eat. Does she give long lectures?"

"They're usually to the point," Mona replied.

I headed toward the PE offices, then spent ten minutes in the area outside Ms. Mahler's den, playing with the straw of my water bottle, waiting to be called in.

"Miss Carvelli."

"Here," I replied and entered.

"All right," she said, sitting down at her desk, shuffling papers. "We would like you to coach the middle school basketball clinic next week, as well as the afternoon camp I told you about. Here is the contract."

I looked at her with surprise. "You're offering me the job?"

"That's right," she said in a matter-of-fact voice. "Hannah is getting tested for mono. We have someone else signed up for the afternoon camp the following week, but if Hannah is still ill, we may need you for sessions after that. I'll keep you posted if you're interested." She studied my face, a small frown forming on hers. "Have you changed your mind?"

"No. No! I'd love to do it. I just didn't think you'd let me after I . . . I guess no one else wanted the basketball job," I said, figuring that was the explanation.

"Actually, two other people did." She handed me a pen across her desk. "If you are referring to the incident," she said, "I have consulted with Josh. At the end of camp yesterday, he said he had a problem with his group and needed to talk to me about it. He didn't use names, he simply told me of the situation. I told him I already knew who was involved—that you had come to see me—and I asked his opinion of hiring you. I usually do not ask my young employees that kind of thing, but in this case, I thought he deserved the right to veto your hiring. He didn't. He said you were very qualified. If you want the job, it's yours."

"I want it. Thank you."

The contract was a list of rules, mostly to do with ensuring the safety of the players and children assigned to me. I agreed to do the afternoon camp as well, signed the papers, and left.

I found Mona in the dining hall with two full trays in front of her.

"I was too nervous to eat," she said.

I sat down.

"Well?"

"She didn't chew me out. That wasn't why she called me in. I got the job," I said. "I got the job, Mona!"

She raised a fist in the air. "Y-yyess!"

"Morning and afternoons."

"Perfect!" She took a huge bite out of her sandwich.

"Mahler gave Josh the chance to veto it, but he didn't."

"I told you," she said, through a mouthful of roast beef, then she chewed and swallowed. "I told you he'd get over it. Josh has always played fair." She took a gulp of soda. "Tell your mother you'll be late getting home next week. Employees are allowed to use the pool after both sessions are over. It's a great cool-down time."

"Do you think I should thank Josh, or keep my distance?"

"I think, whenever you feel like you want to thank someone, you should."

I surveyed the dining hall.

"Except perhaps not at this exact moment," she said, as my eyes locked onto his table.

He was sitting in the corner with three other guys, two of them in Stonegate T-shirts. Melanie was sitting with them, eating an ice-cream cone, taking extra long, luxurious licks.

"Unbelievable," said Mona.

"Yeah, I'm going to change seats, if you don't mind."

"Good idea. Let's look out the window."

We turned our backs to what had to be the hottest table in the room.

"Do you have plans for this weekend?" Mona asked.

I told her about that night's date, and we talked about what I should wear. "You know, one of the really good things about sports," I said, "is that you've got to wear a uniform."

She nodded. "If we didn't, the girls' teams would never make it to the games. We'd keep trying on things, changing our minds. Imagine what the locker room would look like."

I laughed.

"Do you want to get together Sunday and

plan what we're going to do with our basket-ball campers?" Mona proposed.

"Yeah, that would be fun. Do you have a date this weekend?"

"Me? No."

I felt stupid. "Sorry. I've always hated it when people ask me that, because my answer is almost always no."

"No problem," Mona said with a flick of her hand. "I've gotten to the point that I'd rather stay home than go out on another bad date. It seems like all the guys that are cute have noth-ing between the ears. Or they do, but they're babies. Or they're completely stuck on them-selves—that's the worst. It always happens the same way for me. I think I'm dying to get to know a particular guy, then he opens his mouth and ruins it."

"I think that high school guys are probably too young for you," I replied.

"That's what my grandmother says. And then she adds, '*Praise God.*' If I can just survive one more year of Stonegate. . . ."

I was about to tell her she could come to my

dorm on weekends, when I felt someone standing behind us.

Without a word, a ten-dollar bill was dropped over my shoulder and landed on my half-eaten sandwich.

I plucked it from the roll and spun around, but Melanie kept walking.

"Let it go," Mona advised. "She's an idiot. It's not worth arguing with her." Then she smiled. "Way to go, Josh!"

Ten minutes later, after tossing our trash, I headed over to Josh's table. This time, Mona said she would go with me. The four guys stopped talking as we approached the table, which made me feel as if I was in a spotlight.

"Hey, Josh."

"Hey," he acknowledged me, sort of, then turned to his friends. "I guess you all know Monalisa."

They nodded.

"This is Jamie Carvelli." He pointed to the guys, introducing me. "Todd Griffin, Jake Abenoza, Sam Kowalski."

They looked at me with interest, especially the friendly-faced blond guy named Sam.

"I'll just be a second," I said self-consciously.

"We've got fifteen minutes," Sam replied, with an easy kind of smile.

Josh flicked a look at him, and I saw a small shake of the head, as if Josh were discouraging him from asking us to join them.

"I wanted to thank you," I said to Josh. "I know you could have nixed the job."

I paused, because he didn't react, and for a moment I wasn't sure he had heard me.

"I'd have understood if you had vetoed it. But I was really glad to get the job. Thanks."

"Sure." No smile. No warmth in his voice.

"Thanks," I repeated more loudly and earnestly, feeling as if my gratitude was not being accepted.

"Congratulations," he replied, his tone careful and emotionless.

Out of the corner of my eye I saw Mona studying Josh's face, apparently surprised by his response. But I knew what he was saying: His action had been professional, not friendly. He wasn't happy about the fact that I was coming back, but he was—always—a guy who "played fair."

"Well, that's all," I said. "Let's go, Mona."

We left, me walking quickly, Mona looking back over her shoulder.

"It'll be breezy by the waterfront," Mona had said to me later, when we were discussing clothes for the date. "Do you have a skirt that moves? Something short and flirty or long and romantic—a skirt that will do great things in the wind?"

I liked the idea of long and romantic, but all I had was something short and flirty. As it turned out, it won Andrew's approval and seemed like a good choice, even if the skirt was a little difficult to control while walking the promenade of Harborplace and boarding the Seaport Taxi.

The flat-bottomed pontoon boat nosed its way from point to point around the big harbor, to Little Italy, Fells Point, and Canton. City lights reflected in the water. As the boat moved, the tall, glittering buildings of downtown spun slowly around us. There was music drifting out from dockside restaurants and laughter from small boats bobbing around the harbor. After a hot day, the night breeze felt wonderful playing in my hair. Sitting next to Andrew on the boat's wooden bench, I dropped my head back, closed my eyes, and sighed.

I felt his body shift next to me, heard a quiet laugh, then felt him kiss me on my exposed neck. I opened my eyes.

"You like it."

"It's gorgeous. I could ride this boat all night."

He laughed. "You are so—so real, Jamie."

I looked into his blue eyes. I thought it would be nice to be something more romantic sounding than "real," but then he lowered his face and kissed me full on the lips.

I heard a murmur from an older couple sitting across the hull from us, and a titter from some kids toward the back of the boat. I didn't care. I kissed him back.

We got off at Fells Point and walked the narrow, cobblestone streets of the old waterfront. We entered a small shop that sold hand-crafted jewelry. I was leaning over a glass case, looking at earrings, when Andrew opened his hand in front of me to show me a delicate neck-lace. Its string of green stones with small golden beads between them sparkled under the shop's lights. "Try it on," he said, his voice seductive.

He turned me toward an oval mirror on the counter next to us. Standing behind me, he put the necklace around my neck, fastening the clasp, his fingers resting lightly on my shoul-ders.

The color of the stones was perfect for my eyes. I gazed with some amazement at the oval portrait of us reflected in the mirror.

He leaned closer. "Would you let me buy it for you?"

"No."

He laughed softly in my ear, meeting my eyes in the mirror. "I wouldn't have asked, but somehow I knew I should with you."

"You've already bought me dinner and a water taxi pass."

His hands cupped my shoulders.

"Maybe I'll buy it myself," I said.

He moved his mouth closer to my ear. "Let me give it to you," he urged, his voice deep and persuasive. "After all," he whispered, "I'm the one who gets to look at it. I'm the one who gets to see how the beads glisten against your perfect skin."

With one finger, he touched the necklace, sliding the beads lightly against my neck.

"For God's sake, let him buy it!" exclaimed a punky-looking girl, maybe twelve years old, who was watching us.

Andrew laughed, kissed my cheek, then went over to the cashier.

Leaving the shop, we continued down Thames Street, window-shopping and peering in bars, then turned and walked a block away from the water, strolling past tiny eighteenth- and nineteenth-century houses. From time to time, Andrew would stop and gaze down at me, touching the necklace. "You look beautiful in lamplight," he said.

This time, I thought, *I've found someone who is interested in* me. He didn't want a spot on Dad's team. And he certainly didn't want to impress my mother.

We boarded the water taxi again, this time going nowhere in particular, just enjoying the summer breeze and city lights. "Your pass is good for all night," Andrew said, smiling, catching a piece of my blowing hair with his fingers.

"Tell me about your summer job," I said, as the boat puttered on. We had already discussed novels, poetry, and films. If I had taken notes, I could have gotten Advanced Placement in English.

He put his arm around me and we settled back against the railing of the boat.

"I'm a landscaper," he said, "which is not my parents' idea of a smashing summer job."

"What is their idea?" I asked.

"An apprenticeship at an investment firm. A position at a bank. Something one wears a tie to and which doesn't put dirt under one's fingernails."

"But you prefer to be outdoors."

"I prefer honest work. And I enjoy working with my hands," he said.

I looked at the hand cupping my shoulder and noticed that there was no dirt under his fingernails.

"Fluorescent lights and file cabinets don't nurture the soul," he went on. "The earth and sky do. Nature—that's what poets need."

"So you're doing an apprenticeship in land-scaping. You're earning money and learning a skill that will support your writing after college," I said. "Sounds like a good plan to me."

"Oh, I won't be doing this kind of work after college," he said, sounding amused. "I'll go to graduate school."

"Oh, and then teach?"

"Perhaps at a university, where I could write," he replied. "I wouldn't be caught dead teaching high school."

I decided not to remind him that my father did.

"There's a rebel in me," he said, then reached for my face, turning it toward him. "And there's a natural, independent spirit in you. We're good for each other." He played with the necklace, then kissed me again, his mouth pressing against mine.

At that moment fireworks exploded in the air. Above the baseball stadium, I mean. Above Camden Yards, which was close to the waterfront. I remembered that during last night's broadcast they had advertised Fireworks Night, with a display after the game. I wondered if the Orioles had won.

And then I wondered why I was wondering about a baseball game while I was in the middle of a romantic kiss. I sighed, then so did Andrew, but I think it may have been for different reasons. What did it take to send off fireworks in me?

Chapter 14

Saturday morning I woke up at seven. I was tired, but sleepless. After tugging on shorts and a T-shirt, I tiptoed downstairs, carrying my sneakers, hoping that Mom and Viktor were still asleep.

"Good morning!" Viktor was stuffing fruit into a blender.

"G'morning," I mumbled, immediately feeling cross.

"I didn't think you would be up this early," Viktor said.

My thoughts exactly, I felt like responding, then caught myself. Okay, Jamie, he isn't any happier about this arrangement than you are. Give the guy a break. Try to get along.

"I'm tired, but I feel kind of restless. I

thought I'd go out for a walk."

"If I ask you how your date was last night, will you bite my head off?"

"No, I'm not that hungry yet," I said, then laughed. "That was a joke, Viktor. I had a nice time. The harbor was incredible."

He smiled. It was that slow-spreading smile, and maybe if I had seen it without being ready to dislike him as my mother's lover, I would have found it appealing. In Hollywood terms, it was a sexy smile. In my terms, I no longer knew what was sexy or romantic. In the movie world, Andrew would have been *IT*, but the truth was, I had enjoyed kissing that jerk who had wanted to play tight end a lot more. Maybe I expected too much.

"Do you like mangoes?" Viktor asked, studying the array of fruit in front of him.

"I love them, but you should make your juice however you like it."

"I'm happy to share, Jamie," he replied. "I have to get to work, but I'll leave a pitcher chilling in the fridge for you. Take your walk, do some easy stretches, have a juice breakfast, then go back to bed. You put your body through boot camp this week, you have to give those muscles some rest."

He was trying, he really was. I smiled at him. "Thanks, Coach."

I followed Viktor's prescription, and when I woke up at noon, I felt good. I found Mom typing in the little room behind the living room, with Brad and Andrea roosting comfortably outside the window on the AC unit. They cocked their heads and peered in at me as I entered.

"Hi, baby," my mother said. "One more paragraph."

"Don't stop."

"Almost there. Just need him to break this thing off with her," she added.

"Who's breaking things off, Brad?" I asked.

She nodded. "Poor fool. Andrea's rival has conned him. He's wildly in love with Andrea, but has so many self-doubts, that he was ripe for the picking. And Maggie knows it. She wants him just for the money."

"Well, I hope Maggie gets what she deserves in the end."

"Oh, she will," Mom promised. "I've got a big surprise waiting in my outline!"

I picked up a printed sheet that had drifted to the floor, and read through its penciled corrections:

> *His lips drifted onward, careless,* ~~*enticing tantalizing*~~ *teasing?* ~~*leaving her breathless with desire*~~ *making each breath quick and ragged with desire.*

Did Mom write sex scenes from her own experience, I wondered, or did she make most of it up? I set down the page.

"Done. Saved." Mom pushed back from her laptop. "How was last night?"

"It was fun."

"Fun is nice," she said. "Are you going out tonight?"

"No."

She stretched, looking for a moment like a pretty cat, trying to seem casual and uninterested in her prey, but I knew she wanted to pounce with questions. How do you explain to a mother who writes about "breath ragged with desire" that you want to spend Saturday night with a bowl of chips and ESPN?

I watched as Mom stood up, crossed one leg over the other, then bent at the waist, flopping over to touch the floor. Her blonde curls, which had been pulled up on top of her head, bounced around her upside-down face. "Viktor told me I should exercise before and after writing."

"Good idea."

"About Andrew," Mom said, and I stiffened. "Perhaps it's your turn to do the asking, to invite him somewhere. I have a weekend guide —"

"He's doing a poetry reading tonight. He's part of a group scheduled at the Bistro or somewhere."

"Well, then, we could surprise him and go!" she said.

I imagined his face when Mom showed up with her blue alligator purse, jeweled sandals, and the large daisy earrings that were bobbing on her ears at the moment. He'd be surprised all right. "No, I already told him I wasn't coming."

"He asked you, and you said no?"

"A girl doesn't have to accept every invitation, Mom."

"True," she agreed, straightening, her face now right-side up and pink, "but poets are very sensitive about being listened to."

"Everyone likes to be listened to! I don't see why poets have more right than anyone else."

Mom had begun an arm-whirling thing, and the windmill slowed momentarily as she glanced sideways at me.

"Sorry, I didn't meant to snap at you," I said. "Anyway, is there a video store around here?"

"Yes, but how about a girls' night out instead?" she suggested. "Viktor has clients straight through this evening. We could go to a late afternoon movie in Towson, then grab dinner, and do some shopping at the mall. My treat."

She noticed my reluctance. "Or we could just do one of those things," she said.

It wasn't that I was embarrassed to be seen spending Saturday night with my mother. I just wanted to be alone. The past week had been crammed with new people, challenging situations, and feelings so strange I didn't recognize them. Just for a night, I wanted to hibernate from summer in the city.

But I had come crashing into Mom's life, pushed her out of her own office, messed up her writing schedule, and annoyed her boyfriend. And she had been great about it. "I'll drive, if you navigate," I said. "It will help me learn my way around here. Do you have the movie listings?"

Three hours later we set out for Towson, a suburb north of Baltimore and about twenty minutes from Hampden. As I drove in slow circles around a parking garage, we argued over which movie we were going to see. Mom had picked an adventure film she thought I'd be interested in, and I'd chosen a love story that I knew she'd like. The problem was, I wanted to see it, too, but was having trouble admitting it was my first choice.

"Look, Mom," I said at last, "I saw the video of *Sleepless in Seattle* four times. Okay?"

"Baby," she said, "you really are my daughter!"

It sure looked that way by the end of the movie. Mom and I both had the tissues out and emerged into the lobby lights blinking our salty eyes and giggling self-consciously.

"There's nothing like tragic love to make me hungry," Mom said. "What are you in the mood for?"

"What do you they have around here?"

"Everything. Sushi, Italian, seafood . . . junk food at the mall's food court," she added with a conspiratorial smile.

"A food court with a place that sells giant-size chocolate chip cookies?"

"The chips are as big as quarters."

"Let's go."

We got Chinese from the food court and decided to shop before dessert. I had thought my friend Abby was the US gold medalist in shopping, but comparing her to my mother was like comparing a 5K runner to a marathoner.

Abby shopped for herself and sometimes for me, picking out stuff she thought I should try on. My mother shopped for herself, me, and her characters.

"This is just what Maggie would wear!" she said, holding up loungewear that no other teen's mother would have held up to her daughter. She had coaxed me into Victoria's Secret and insisted on buying me something. I knew I'd never be able to sleep in the lacy nightie she was eyeing for me. I ended up leaving the store with a bra and panties so sexy, when I wore them I'd probably blush just remembering what I had on underneath. We picked out dishes and barware for Brad at Crate&Barrel, then found shoes for Andrea at Nordstrom's. Mom couldn't resist fancy soap from Crabtree & Evelyn — like we didn't have enough at home already. Then we went to Hecht's, and Mom pointed out furniture for the woman who had been sitting two tables away from us at the food court. That bit of interior decorating had begun with my simple observation that the woman's date looked kind of grumpy. My mother had then spun out an entire story line about their past and present together, as well as this woman's future. Now the woman had a roomful of furniture to go with the new life Mom had developed for her. For Rita Carvelli, shopping wasn't just about buying things, it was a creative experience.

Finally back at the food court, with just twenty minutes before the mall shut down, we collapsed onto plastic chairs, munching on large chocolate chip cookies and sipping coffee. I felt an unexpected kind of contentment. Somehow, during the course of the last six hours, moments of silence had become relaxed.

My mother sat back in her chair and sighed happily. Then I saw her surveying the food court.

"Looking for more characters? You should try airports, Mom."

"Inspiration is everywhere," she said. "I am getting better at seeing it in the quiet ones, people who go about their everyday life with secret dreams."

I set down my latte. "I guess we all have them."

"If you're human, you have them," she replied. "What do you think Ted's secret dreams are?"

"Ted's?"

"He carries the dreams his parents have for him, of course. I think it must be hard to be a child of achieving parents."

I sipped and thought about him. "Now you've got me curious."

"But not interested," my mother observed, and took a bite of her cookie.

"What do you mean?"

"Not romantically interested."

"In Ted? He's a friend. I can't imagine me getting romantic about him, or him about me. He's a fantastic guy, and I know he'd be great for some girl, but him and me? I can't even picture it. Besides, I left behind a million guy-friends who like to talk sports. I want . . . something different."

"Like Andrew," my mother replied.

I didn't want to discuss him with her, so I

kept to a definition. "Like someone who makes me tingle, someone who sees me in a crowd of people and thinks"—I hesitated, feeling silly saying something I couldn't imagine actually happening to me—"thinks about something other than the fact that he'd like to be on my father's team, or he'd like to have me on his team in a pick-up game."

My mother gazed at me thoughtfully. "Someone who looks in your eyes and feels his heart hammering against his ribs?" she suggested. "Someone who thinks that he would give anything to hold you in his arms? Someone who thinks that he would die to kiss you?"

"That sounds good," I said, grimacing with the effort to imagine it.

"You're cynical about love."

I shrugged. "Maybe."

"Because of your father and me?" she asked.

"What do you mean?"

"Because ours didn't last."

"No," I replied. "No, that's really not it. I've just had some bad luck with guys, and when it blows up in your face, it's miserable. Actually, it hasn't been much better for my friends. I don't know why it should be so hard for two people to fall in love and stay in love for more than a week. It seems like romance should happen naturally or something, but I find sports a lot easier."

"Well," she said, "Andrew certainly knows how to woo a girl."

I detected the dry note in her voice. "Was that a put-down?"

"An observation, baby, just an observation. He seems very romantic. I can understand why you'd want to go out with him."

Could she understand why I felt like an actress in a romantic film rather than a girl actually falling for a guy? Maybe I expected too much too soon. Maybe I just had to play the part for a while and wait for it to happen. "I guess that, for some people, love grows slowly," I said.

My mother nodded. "Some people fall head over heels. Other people begin to fall without even knowing it—love grows like a spring flower beneath last autumn's leaves and catches them by surprise. I plot it both ways in my books."

"Well, you're the expert," I said, then saw a grimace on *her* face.

"On paper," she replied, "on paper."

Chapter 15

When we arrived home that night, there was a message from Ted on the answering machine. "Hey, Jamie. I'm painting the living room tomorrow, so I'll have the game on inside. If you can stand the smell of paint and are just hanging out, come over." I saw the disappointment on Mom's face when she heard Ted's voice, and I knew she had hoped it was Viktor.

Nine o'clock Sunday morning Viktor arrived and settled into making breakfast, fussing over my mother, insisting that she put her feet up and read the paper. When I asked him for one of his juice concoctions, he made a pleased fuss over that, too.

Mona drove up at eleven thirty and we walked to The Avenue. Her hair was pulled back as usual, showing off her gorgeous eyes and cheekbones, but today her long braids were uncoiled, swinging loose down her back, dancing whenever she laughed. From a shop called Oh, Said Rose, she bought earrings that also swung. We tried on vintage hats at Fat Elvis, then I squeezed my feet into several pairs of fabulous slip-ons at Ma Petite Shoe, but we only bought truffles there—the store sold shoes and chocolate—what more could a girl want?

During a late lunch at Café Hon, Mona pulled from her bag several copies of coaching schedules that had been used at the basketball camps in previous years. Each of us was assigned ten players who would be entering sixth to eighth grade, but that didn't tell us as much as we'd need to know to decide on drills and teaching points. We talked through all the possibilities so that we would be ready for whatever level of player showed up.

While Mona and I were working with middle school girls, Todd and Jake, two of the guys who I'd met through Josh on Friday, would be coaching middle school boys in basketball. Josh and Sam, the friendly blond guy, would be running the lacrosse camp for middle school boys.

"Sam is Josh's teammate at Hopkins," Mona informed me. "He's a defenseman—Josh says he's aggressive and a wild man on the field, but a marshmallow off."

The six of us, plus two more girls, would be working the weeklong afternoon camp with elementary school kids, grades two though five. The coaches and counselors had met before lacrosse camp, so Ms. Mahler had given Mona the notes from that meeting and asked her to go over them with me. Another eight A.M. meeting was scheduled Monday to straighten out any last-minute problems. I was excited and couldn't wait to tell Dad the news that his baby girl was coaching.

Mona and I were eating after the peak lunch hour, so we sat at our table for a long time, unrushed by the waitress, stirring the crushed ice in our glasses and talking. We switched from camp and sports to college hopes.

"So, what's the status with Andrew?" she asked.

"We were talking about colleges," I replied.

"Well, he's a college guy," she reasoned. "But

even if he wasn't, I wouldn't let you off the hook that easily. Friday, you had plans for the most romantic date gone on by any girl I actually know, and"—she looked at her watch—"since we started down The Avenue more than three hours ago, you haven't mentioned it."

"It was fun."

She rolled her eyes. "I guess you didn't inherit your mother's skill for details. I bought one of her books and started it Friday night."

When Mona arrived at the house, she and my mother had hit it off immediately, just as Josh and Mom had. For some reason, Mom could get away with asking my friends questions that other parents couldn't. Maybe it was her tone—intrigued rather than judgmental—like she was researching a story.

"We ate at The Rusty Scupper," I said, then thought to add a detail, "a window table. We walked some streets in Fells Point—they were cobblestone. Later on we saw fireworks over Camden Yards. It was a Friday night promotion by the Orioles."

"Girlfriend, that's a travel article, not a romance."

I fingered my green stone necklace. "I got this at Fells Point."

"It's awesome with your eyes! So, did he give it to you or did you buy it yourself?"

"I wanted to buy it myself, but he gave it to me."

Mona sighed. "Maybe you're traveling to romance, but you sure aren't there yet. Is there any chance of me getting a look at this guy?"

"Well, Ted's home today, painting, and said to come over and hang out if I wanted."

"Ted is your stoop-sitting buddy, Andrew's roommate?"

I nodded. "So we can hang out and see if Andrew passes through."

Mona studied me, her long fingers playing with one of her earrings. "You don't sound very enthusiastic."

"Oh, Ted's great. And he'll have the game on. I think Cabrera is pitching today."

She laughed. "I've got to tell you, I'm not sure you're even *traveling* to romance, at least when it comes to Andrew."

I blushed.

"Want to spill it?" she asked.

Despite two refills, there was no ice left to stir in my glass. "Spill what?"

"Spill whatever is in your gut, whatever is making you hesitate when you answer my questions."

I stared at my empty glass, then made a stab at explaining. "Sometimes I think that love is one big fairy tale. I wonder if people who say they are in love, if—really—they've just talked themselves into it. They want it so badly, they kind of make it happen. They fake it until they start believing their own story. Maybe that's just sour grapes or something. Maybe because it doesn't happen to me, I don't want to think it happens to anybody else. You're not arguing with me, Mona," I said. "Tell me I'm wrong about love."

She shook her head. "I started wondering the same thing about a year ago. I feel like I'm missing some kind of love gene. I think I'm falling for a guy, then he opens his mouth, and the spell is broken. I mean, if I find a handsome frog, the one thing I should *not* do is kiss it, because the frog will become a prince, and that prince will talk, and then I'll want to dump him back in the pond!"

I laughed out loud, picturing Mona in a princess outfit, heaving a crowned jock into a swamp.

"Another iced tea, hon?" the waitress asked Mona, then me. We glanced at each other.

"No, no thanks," Mona replied, then scooped up the camp materials she had spread on the table between us and stuffed them in her bag. "We'll just take the check." To me she said, "Well, now that we've gotten each other totally depressed, I guess we should go home. I'd still like a peek at Andrew. It would be fun to see what a walking romance character looks like. And we can check the baseball score with Ted."

We left money for our food and a tip. By the time we reached my house, our bladders were bursting, and we raced upstairs to the bathroom, leaving Viktor flattened against the hallway wall and laughing. Then we headed next door.

I could hear the broadcast of the game and smell the fresh paint through the front screen door. "Hey, Ted," I called, peering in. "Is it safe to come in?"

"It's your head more than your feet you've got to worry about. You could end up looking like some pigeons have passed over."

Behind me, Mona laughed.

"I've got to keep going for a moment, don't want to lose my place," Ted added.

Opening the door, I saw that he was on a ladder, painting a careful edge with a brush and shield at the corner of the ten-foot-high ceiling.

"I've brought Monalisa, my teammate from camp."

"Hi, Monalisa," he said, his back still turned to us, his focus on the strokes he was making where the ceiling met the wall. "Have a seat, but check it for paint splatters first. You might get polka dots on your behinds."

Mona laughed again and we checked out the sofa. "You know," I said, "this old couch looks better with the sheet on it."

"No kidding!" He lowered his arms, examining the job he had just done. "The Orioles are winning . . . barely. Cabrera hasn't had his stuff today, but—" he turned to look at us.

"But?" I said.

"But, uh, he was, uh —"

"Yeah?"

"Able to, uh —"

I waited a little impatiently as Ted stood above us, seeming unable to complete his sentence. In fact, he appeared unable to move and totally unaware that he was holding onto a wet brush rather than the ladder.

"Do you think you should put down that brush?" I suggested.

He glanced down at it. "Good idea."

After placing the brush carefully on the paint tray, he turned back to us. "Hi." The shy greeting was directed to Mona.

"Hi," she replied in an equally soft voice.

"But Cabrera was able to what?" I asked, hoping Ted would finish his sentence.

"Uh, get out of the inning, I think. Yes. Twice, with the bases loaded."

"Can you take a break, Ted?" I asked. "I think you've been standing near the ceiling too long."

He glanced toward the ceiling, then descended the ladder and crossed the room. "I'm

Ted," he said to Mona and held out his hand. Mona shook it, as if she hadn't noticed the paint on it, and maybe she hadn't, for the next moment, they both looked down with surprise at their wet palms.

"Oh, sorry!" Ted said. "That was dumb, I'm sorry!" He glanced around, looking for a rag. "Here, wipe it off," he said, offering his shirt, which, like all of Ted's clothes, was sparkling clean, not a speck of paint on it.

"But I'll ruin it," Mona said.

He wiped his own hand on his shirt. "Now it's okay," he told her.

Mona laughed, then wiped her hand on his shirt as well.

What was wrong with him? I wondered. Either he had been inhaling paint fumes or — no, no, not him, not her. It couldn't be!

Chapter 16

"So you're Jamie's teammate," Ted said.

"Yes," replied Mona.

"You, uh, are going to be coaching . . . basketball," he remembered.

"Yes," Mona said. "Both Jamie and I."

"You, uh, play . . . lacrosse."

Spit it out, Ted, I thought grouchily.

"Yes," Mona replied sweetly.

"Jamie says you're fantastic at it."

"Yes . . . I mean, no!" Mona said, catching herself. "I play okay."

Now I was wondering about *her*. What happened to wanting to dump a frog prince in a pond when he opened his mouth and had nothing to say? Not that Ted wasn't fun to talk to, but at that exact moment he sounded like he was recovering from severe head trauma.

"So, would you like some iced tea?" Ted asked.

"Thanks, but if we drink any more—" I began.

"I'd love it," said Mona.

Ted smiled. "I grow my own mint. And I make mint tea. From my mint," he said.

"Cool!" Mona turned to me. "Let's try some."

"Already have," I replied, then felt bad for my short answer. "But why not—it's great."

She and I followed Ted toward the back of the house.

"Hey, it sounds like the Orioles just hit a homer," I called to them, suddenly hearing the roar of the crowd on Ted's radio, and backing up to learn the details. Mona and Ted kept going. Sighing, I listened for the info and score, then joined them in the kitchen.

"It was."

"Sorry?" Ted said.

"The Orioles. You know, Baltimore's baseball team, the one you listen to every day, and

Brian Roberts, one of your two favorite players—he just hit a three-run homer to put the Orioles ahead."

"Good," said Ted.

Had this been yesterday, we would have been dancing around, high-fiving.

"I didn't know you were a baseball fan," Mona said to me, momentarily becoming herself again.

"I told you I like to listen to games with Ted."

I saw caution seep into her eyes. She glanced away, and I knew she was trying to remember everything I had said about Ted, then she focused on me again, as if trying to read my face.

No, no, no! I felt like screaming at her. He's just a friend. I don't want him to be anything else!

And I really didn't, but I also didn't want *her* to think of him as anything else. I was used to losing my guy buddies to another girl and could handle that just fine; they usually drifted back when it was all over. It was Mona I didn't want to lose. I had finally found a soul mate, a girl who was really interested in guys and who dreamed about romance, but who also thought that finding such a thing might be more difficult than earning Olympic gold. For fifteen minutes I was friends with someone who knew exactly how that felt, and now she was gone.

Of course, I knew how selfish and stupid I was being.

"So what school do you go to?" Ted asked Mona.

She hesitated, and I guessed that she didn't want to admit to being in high school.

"Stonegate," she said at last.

He nodded. "Off Lehman Avenue, where the camp is."

"Yes."

"Will you be a senior?" he asked hopefully.

"Yes."

Good thing Ted never said that he wanted to dump a princess who couldn't carry a conversation, the rotten part of me thought.

"So, uh, what position do you play in lacrosse?"

"Midfielder."

Ted was impressed, I could see it on his face, because midfielders—which is what Josh was—did it all, defend, pass, shoot.

Be a friend, Jamie, I told myself. "You ought to see her play, Ted. She's faster than anybody, and a great shooter."

"I'd like to," replied Ted, so earnestly, that for a second I wished I hadn't said anything. If there was anyone who would be able to see all of Mona's beauty, not just how she looked standing still, but her beauty in motion, it was a sports fan like him. I could picture the scene, the awed expression Ted would get on his face watching her play. He'd end up restricted to little more than a string of short sentences. Mona would leave him breathless. Why couldn't I ever leave a guy breathless?

As we sat down at the kitchen table and sipped our iced teas—they sipped, I played with the sweat rings from my glass—the interview continued. They were curious about each other, but had a funny, almost charming shyness about saying or asking too much. When necessary, I filled in the awkward silences. I grew increasingly desperate to leave, but I wanted to be a friend and couldn't think how to exit and, at the same time, encourage Mona to stay. While I was searching for an excuse, the back door opened.

"Well, hello," Andrew said, looking surprised to see Mona and me. To his roommate he added teasingly, "And I was feeling guilty about leaving you home with the paint job. Next time, I'll volunteer to do the ceiling."

"You must be Andrew," Mona observed. I saw her assessing him, as if she had finally recalled why we first came over. Andrew saw it, too, and seemed to take her interest as flattering. Ted saw Andrew's reaction and began to look tense; he was afraid Andrew would impress Mona.

Well, he'd never worried about that with me, I thought. Why couldn't a guy ever look at me and Andrew together, then want to strangle Andrew just for showing up?

"And you are?" Andrew asked his appraiser.

"Monalisa Devine."

"Monalisa Devine," he repeated, enjoying her name. "Two trochees and an iamb."

"Excuse me?"

"Andrew is a poet," Ted explained.

"Trochees and iambs are metrical feet in poetry—a description of rhythm," Andrew said. "You have an inspired name."

"My grandmother gave it to me."

"As a birth gift," Andrew guessed. "She wanted to ensure that you would be as beautiful and mysterious as DaVinci's woman."

Mona raised one eyebrow. "Actually, she was a fan of Nat King Cole, and 'Mona Lisa' was her favorite song."

Ted laughed—a little too loudly, I thought.

"How clever of her," Andrew remarked.

"Listen, Mona," I said, "I forgot that I told my dad I'd call him—" I glanced at my watch—"between three thirty and four, and he'll be disappointed if I don't. But why don't you stay and hang out?"

"Well," she said, sounding indecisive for the first time since I'd known her, probably the first time in her life.

"May I have the honor of walking you home, Miss?" Andrew asked me gallantly. "We'll take the long way," he said, smiling and pulling my arm through the crook of his, guiding me out of the kitchen and toward the front of the house.

Passing through the living room, he eyed the open can, the brush with paint drying on it, and the unfinished ceiling. When we got outside, he asked, "Did I see what I think I did?"

"What do you think you saw?"

"Is something hot going on between them?"

"I don't know," I said, for some reason unwilling to share the details that I was mulling over in my own mind. "They've known each other for only forty-five minutes."

Andrew smiled a different kind of smile than before, a sexy smile. "We've known each other for only a week. Things can happen fast. I missed you last night."

"Did you?"

He looked into my eyes. "Very much." He put his arm around my shoulder and led me in the opposite direction from my house, toward The Avenue. "The long route," he reminded me, "at least around the block. Perhaps we could take a ride in my Jeep with the top down. It's parked in the back."

We walked in silence, his arm keeping me close. We must have made a striking pair—on The Avenue, people turned to gaze at us, and not in the usual way people look at me because I'm tall.

"Last night," said Andrew, "I gave my most powerful reading ever, and I wished you were there for it."

"I—well, maybe the next one," I said.

"Afterward, people kept coming up to me, giving me compliments," he went on. "They were really moved by the last two poems I read, the women especially. Or perhaps women are simply more comfortable about expressing their feelings and responding passionately to a poet. It can go to your head, Jamie."

I thought, *Perhaps, it already has.*

"I'm glad it was such a great experience," I said aloud.

"It would have been perfect if you had been there. What did you do instead?" he asked.

There's nothing like bottled-up irritation to make you say things you wouldn't normally say. "I shopped at Victoria's Secret."

His eyes widened. "Really!"

"I hope the weather is cooler tomorrow," I said, changing the subject before I was asked to supply details.

"May I see you tomorrow night?" Andrew asked.

"Well, it's my first day of camp, my first day of coaching."

"You're coaching?"

"Yes, I told you about it, remember? I'm coaching basketball in the morning and working as a camp counselor in the afternoon. I'm so excited!"

"I thought you were attending a lacrosse camp," he said.

"That ended Friday, remember?"

He didn't, I knew from the expression on his face, but I clearly recalled squeezing in an account of the last day of lacrosse as the waiter served our dinner salads and slipping in a brief description of my new job while we window-shopped in Fells Point.

"Sometimes you—just gazing in your eyes makes me very distracted," he said.

"Oh."

We turned the corner and I saw his Jeep parked against the backyard fence.

"It's sizzling in the city," he whispered. "Why don't we find some cool country roads?"

Like a boat ride on a glittering city night, a drive with the Jeep's top down on a summery country day was an incredibly seductive idea.

"I'd love it!"

"The seats are going to be hot," he warned, "but at least they're real leather and won't stick to you like those of a cheap car. Here, you can use my shirt." He opened the door on the passenger side, then removed his Tommy Hilfiger and spread it on the seat. He must have done his landscape work shirtless, or else he used a tanning salon, for there were no shirtsleeve or collar lines on his smoothly tanned body. I enjoyed looking at him and wondered to myself if some of the ladies who hired him for "private contracting" did as well.

Settled happily in my seat, I enjoyed the start and stop of little breezes as we maneuvered through the city traffic lights, heading north, eventually passing the mall where my mother and I had shopped. About a half mile past it, the road became much greener, and began to dip and rise. I lay my head back against the soft leather seat, gazed up at the sky and the trees passing overhead, and sighed.

I heard Andrew laugh deep in his throat, then he reached for my hand. He slowly brought it to his mouth and kissed my fingers. We drove past horse farms—through steeplechase country, according to signs—and the rolling hills and drifts of wildflowers seemed to affect my head like wine. Now and then we passed beneath a tunnel of trees. Underneath a willow, Andrew pulled off the road.

"I don't think you have to be a poet," I told him. "I think that nature nurtures even ordinary girls like me."

"You're not ordinary, Jamie," he replied.

I blushed.

"How could you be?" he added. "I would never fall for an ordinary girl." Then his lips touched mine and he showered my face with light kisses. "Let's sit on the grass," he murmured between kisses.

He pulled a blanket off the backseat and spread it beneath the willow, with the Jeep shielding us from view of the road. Sitting on the soft cloth, he pulled me down with him.

As he started to kiss me again, I thought, *If he had a blanket in his Jeep, he didn't need to take off his shirt* —which, I guess, was sort of unromantic of me to notice.

Andrew kissed my eyelids, then each ear. I felt his hands in my hair, expertly loosening it from its fasteners, taking it down slowly. Not like the guys at home, I thought, who rushed from a light kiss to an all-out effort, with no interest in warming up.

Andrew's fingers lifted my hair and let it ripple. "My lioness!" he whispered.

The next moment I was flat on my back. So much for warming up.

I guess he didn't need to—he was hot, very hot—in fact, his skin was sticky all over, and his kiss wet and smeary. I was totally turned off. Feeling his full weight on top of me, I knew I had to get him off.

"I don't think I'm ready for this," I said. *With you, I don't think I'll ever be ready*, I thought.

"Jamie, I want you so badly."

"I'm sorry, I'm not here for that."

"All last night, I lay in bed thinking of you—"

"This is the side of a road, and I don't want anything more than a kiss."

"—I lay dreaming of you, longing for you, for your touch, for your scent, for your—"

I'd heard enough, and I had made what I wanted perfectly clear. I gave him a powerful shove. Maybe he forgot what kind of girl he was on top of. He landed on the ground next to me with a thump and a surprised look on his face. But he recovered quickly.

"I came on too fast," he said. "You work such magic, Jamie. I couldn't resist, I just couldn't help myself. I hope I didn't scare you."

"No, you didn't scare me."

"I'll move more slowly the next time," he promised.

What next time? I thought.

He reached over to play with a strand of my hair. "You're incredible. You're like some kind of wild Atalanta," he said, then smiled at me. "You're familiar with mythology, I assume?"

Oh, great, here comes the lit lesson.

Oh, why, why, why couldn't I get romantic? A romantic girl would have smiled encouragingly. She would have made him feel smart as he taught her mythology. She would have waited eagerly for him to explain the compliment he wanted to give her. I tried smiling, but I thought that Andrew had to see it was fake.

If he did, it didn't stop him. "Atalanta was a beautiful huntress, who could shoot and wrestle with the best of men, and outrun them all. She had many suitors, and she held on to her freedom and wild forays in the forest by insisting that the only man she would marry was the one who could beat her in a footrace. For a time, she enjoyed countless races with handsome youths, winning them all. Then she met her match, a young man name Melanion. He appealed to Aphrodite, the goddess of love, who gave him three golden apples. As he raced Atalanta, he rolled the apples past her, one by one, each one a little farther off course. Because she stooped to pick them up, he won, and won her as his own. Eventually, he and she were turned into lions."

Andrew stopped as if waiting for me to respond.

"She should have kept her eye on the finish line," I said, "and then gone back for the apples."

"Perhaps," said Andrew, an edge in his voice, "she saw it as her one and only chance."

"If she was that good an athlete," I persisted, "she should have had the confidence and discipline to pull off both."

Andrew's blue eyes sparked, and I thought he was going to argue back, then his gaze mellowed into something like that of a parent smiling at a wayward but amusing child, which really annoyed me.

"I should get home," I said. "My dad is probably pretty upset that I haven't called him yet."

"Your dad? I thought calling him was just an excuse."

Exactly, I felt like replying, but I just smiled.

After helping Andrew fold up the blanket, I climbed into the Jeep and buckled my seat belt for a long ride back.

Chapter 17

Mona called that night.

"Jamie," she said, "be honest. Should I apologize?"

"For what?" I asked.

"For . . . for moving in on your territory."

I stretched out on my leopard-skin spread. "I don't want to date Ted, I really don't, Mona, though I think he's one of the greatest guys around."

"Still," she said, "he's your friend."

"So are you," I replied.

"Sometimes three's a crowd. It changes things," she added quietly.

"Change can be good. It just depends on what we make of it."

It was as if Mona was saying all the "bad

Jamie" thoughts and I was countering with the "good Jamie" thoughts.

"He is so damn gorgeous!" she said.

I reached for the rose my Baltimore Hon had given me, sticking it my hair. "He has a brain and a heart, too," I said, "though I don't know if the brain showed up before you went home today." I lay on my back and put my bare feet up on the wall. "Did you guys start talking in actual sentences?"

She laughed. "It's not just what a person says."

"Tell that to the princes you dumped in the pond."

She laughed loudly, then grew serious. "What about his parents?"

"What about them?"

"Are they liberal or conservative?" she asked.

I removed the rose from my hair, and ran its satin softness over my cheek. "I don't know— who cares? Do you want to date *them*?"

"Jamie, get real," she said firmly. "I am not Chinese. Or blonde."

"So how about your grandmother?" I asked.

"Is she liberal or conservative?"

"Politically, she's liberal. When it comes to family, she's very conservative, but I can handle that."

"And so can Ted," I pointed out.

There was a long silence. "Of course, I don't even know if he's interested. . . ."

"Mona, get real," I said, as firmly as she had.

We signed off a few minutes later, promising to meet at seven forty-five the next morning outside the PE offices.

Then I called Dad and told him the news about coaching a basketball clinic. He got a huge kick out of it and wanted to hear all about the things I'd learned at lacrosse camp. (I left out the lesson about making bets.) Throughout the conversation he kept saying, "It's good to talk to you, Jamie. It's good to talk to you, Jamie," so often I started feeling bad for waiting a week to call. After my first call from Baltimore, I had decided not to phone for a few days, figuring I'd never get independent if I called every time I missed him. Then a few days became a week. I missed him a lot, but I was anything but lonely or unhappy, and that was an amazing thing to discover.

While I was on the phone with Dad, I heard Mom and Viktor arguing downstairs. Their voices grew quiet just as I hung up, so I waited five minutes, then went downstairs to get some ice cream. Big mistake! Mom and Viktor were making up—and I don't mean with a warm little hug. I tiptoed back up the stairs, my face on fire.

I felt surrounded—surrounded by lovers. Even my so-called bedroom wasn't a retreat, with Mom's Post-its stuck on the walls and furniture. Trapped in it, with nothing but a library of romances, I felt like tying bedsheets together and climbing out the window. I needed ESPN— or maybe Stephen King—sports or horror, either would do. If I'd had any guts, I'd have walked downstairs, right past them, and driven off to Barnes & Noble, which I had seen somewhere near the mall. But I stayed where I was, glowering at the collection of old fairy tale books stacked by my bed. Having nothing else to do, I paged through them.

Finally, I fell asleep and started dreaming. In the dream I was half-asleep, trapped in a castle surrounded by briars. I heard the buzz of an electric hedge trimmer. Someone was cutting his way toward me. At last, he leaped through the window — Andrew, wielding an orange trimmer with an incredibly long extension cord. On his back was a huge sack. He rushed to my bed and in a flash I saw what was written on the sack — MANURE. He was going to bury me in it! I rose from my bed and ran all the way to the end of the dream.

When I awoke Monday morning, I was still wearing my clothes from the day before. One of my fairy tale books was in bed with me, opened to the page of Sleeping Beauty being kissed by her prince. On my pillow, next to where I had laid my head, rested the pink satin rose I had received from my Baltimore Hon. Although I knew I must have put it there, I couldn't remember doing it, and it felt as if it had been placed there for me as a sign. The rose held a kind of magic, a magic I almost believed in, left for me by a guy with no purpose but to be sweet and to remind me that he had tripped over a curb for me.

Having dawdled in bed, I hurried to the bathroom for a fast shower, raced down to the kitchen and gulped one of Viktor's specials, then headed for Stonegate. Mona arrived in the parking lot at the same time as I did. We walked together toward the PE offices, me lugging my girl's lacrosse stick, field shoes, tennis racket, and a bag stuffed with a bathing suit, towel, and slides. Mona and I had a lot of plans for after work this week and the weeks following, and I really hoped that those plans would not disappear completely now that she had met Ted. I could just see me playing tennis with Ms. Mahler.

Crossing the fields that were on the way to the PE building, we saw two guys playing lacrosse. Even from a distance, and even though I had only seen him in action as an opposing player the first day, I knew immediately the attacker was Josh.

"We're early," Mona said, glancing at her big-faced watch, then veering toward the lacrosse field. As we got closer I saw the other player was the big blond guy named Sam Kowalski, the one with the easy smile, Josh's teammate at Hopkins. Sam and Josh were heckling each other. I heard the same laughter and saw the same playfulness that had surprised me the day Josh showed up for Mom's autograph.

"Sam's great," Mona told me as we watched. "Even though he's a defender, he can shoot."

I nodded, but my eyes were on Josh. I remembered Andrew's description of the basketball game between Josh and me as a kind of ballet. Josh had the strength and grace of an incredible dancer, seeming to negate gravity as he extended himself straight out or suddenly leaped up to snag a ball, being able to pivot and shift directions, his balance always perfect, sometimes defying what seemed physically possible.

"Josh is awesome," I breathed.

Mona turned to me. "Praise God! I thought you would never see it."

I quickly glanced at her. "I mean as a player."

She studied my face for a moment, then said, "You ought to see him in a real game."

"Yeah, I know. Ted said he was great."

Mona's eyes lit up. "What else did Ted say?"

Oh, no, I thought. *Here we go.* I had mentioned Ted as a way of covering what might have sounded like a girl's lust for a jock. Now I had awakened Mona's hunger for details about Ted.

"Well, I think he said that Josh is a real team player."

"Yes," said Mona.

"And that they were in Chem lab together."

"Really," Mona replied.

"Josh said they had a lousy instructor, so everybody went to Ted for help."

"Wow."

Apparently Mona was restricted to single words again, and impressed by almost anything to do with Ted. "He's really smart, as well as really nice," I added.

"Yes."

"Monalisa, you've gone right off the edge."

"I know," she said with a frown.

At that moment, Sam and Josh spotted us.

"Hey," said Sam, waving his stick at us. "Two against two?"

Josh said something to his buddy, which

made him look at his watch and give a little shrug.

"My stick's in my locker," Mona called back.

"Later, then," said Sam.

"I don't think Josh wants to play with me," I told Mona as we continued on to the PE offices.

"You're too sensitive, girl," she replied.

Todd and Jake were already in the outer office of the PE building, reviewing their plans for the middle school boys' basketball camp. A petite redhead wearing funky earrings and an odd mix of bracelets introduced herself as Caitlin. "I'll be doing a group in the afternoon," she said. "Noelle and I are going to help Ms. Mahler organize things this morning while everybody else coaches."

"Caitlin is our school's best artist," Mona said, which made Caitlin blush. "She's also the girl who turns the pinkest the fastest."

"Keep it up, braids," Caitlin replied, which shocked me a little.

Mona pinched Caitlin's cheek, and Caitlin

yanked one of Mona's loose braids, then they both laughed.

"We've been going to Stonegate together since kindergarten," Mona said. "Can you tell?"

Another girl arrived.

"Noelle! How were the old folks?" Mona asked.

"Noelle has the *misfortune* of having two sets of grandparents in Hawaii," Caitlin explained to me.

The girl looked Hawaiian, with shimmering black hair and a face that should have been wreathed in white flowers.

"This is Jamie. She's new to Baltimore, and," Mona said, pausing to create drama, "she's a Lady Terp. Got a basketball scholarship."

Noelle smiled a stunning smile. "I'm at Maryland, just finished my freshman year."

Josh and Sam arrived, grinning, sweaty, with towels around their necks, looking very cute. Jocks—guy jocks, that is—often have that talent for looking sweaty and cute. The big M emerged from her office.

"Let's begin," she said, without any other

kind of greeting. It was precisely eight o'clock and she had her clipboard in hand.

We took seats on the long sofas against the walls and, interestingly, divided up into guys on one side, girls on the other. Some things you never outgrow. Ms. Mahler handed out our coaching rosters, then the rosters for the afternoon camp. We began to review the schedule, which rotated the second, third, fourth, and fifth grades through three basic kinds of activities: sports, arts, and library. We were paired up, a boy and girl counselor for each grade, with twenty kids between us.

Sam raised his hand. "I think you have me with the wrong group," he said. "At our first meeting, you assigned me to second grade."

"That's right," Noelle added, when Ms. Mahler didn't respond right away. "Sam and I are supposed to do second grade. Josh was supposed to do third with Hannah, and he's with Jamie now."

"That was a preliminary schedule," Ms. Mahler replied. "This is the final one."

The Big M was smooth, but that didn't keep Noelle and Sam from looking puzzled, then looking at Josh, who kept his eyes on the paper before him. He had asked her to change the schedule—I knew it immediately. Everyone looked from him to me, and I felt my cheeks getting pink—pinker than Caitlin's. I think my ears were blushing, too.

Ms. Mahler marched on through her clipboard notes. As soon as the meeting was over, Mona started talking basketball to me, providing a kind of escort out of the room. She was thoughtful enough not to make a comment about the situation, or worse, try to give it a positive spin.

By the time I saw my collection of kids assembled on the gym bleachers—tall, short, skinny, fat, some nervous, one overly confident, several gigglers, and one who looked like she was going to cry—I forgot about feeling hurt. For three hours I was in my own world, already doing what I had always hoped I would do after college. *And they call this work?* I thought, even though I knew from Dad that coaching was work when it came down to doing it day after day. But it was such a blast!

Some girls were good shooters, others

couldn't have hit the side of a barn. All of them needed to work on ball-handling skills, except one Energizer Bunny, who wanted to hog the ball and play straight through my stop-play whistles. Athletically talented, driven to succeed, and determined to finish whatever she started, she was cocky enough to be labeled as "trouble"—and as I walked to lunch with Mona, I wondered if that was how Josh saw me.

At lunch, I sat between Mona and Noelle. The four guys sat across from the four girls, with Sam directly across from me and Josh grabbing the chair at the far end of the table. Sam kept us entertained with jokes and funny stories, and although he was teasing and laughing with all of us, I couldn't help but notice that his eyes kept drifting back to Noelle. When he stood up to get a second ice cream, I got up with him.

"Want me to bring you one?" he asked.

"I'm not sure what I want yet," I replied, and when we were finally out of earshot of the others, I added, "Actually, I just want to say I'm sorry."

"For what?"

"For messing up the schedule. I'm sorry

you got stuck with me."

"I'm not sorry," he said, but I didn't believe him.

He glanced back toward the table. "I'm pretty obvious, aren't I?" he added in a quieter voice. "Maybe I should sit on the same side as Noelle from now on, so I don't keep looking across at her. She had a boyfriend last year, but I heard she broke up with him."

"I'm sorry I took away your golden opportunity."

"It might be better this way," Sam reasoned. "I mean, that would have been just more opportunity for me to screw up, right? You and I, we're going to have a great time together. And besides, Jamie, you're not responsible for the schedule."

"I'm responsible for Josh asking for a change in it. I'm sure he did."

Sam looked as if he were going to deny it, then decided otherwise. "The problem with Josh is that lacrosse — all sports, really — come way too easy to him. And school is the same way. But there are a few things that don't. When someone is as successful as he is, we expect him to handle everything well, but he doesn't. I recommend the Eskimo cones."

I bought one and returned to the table with him. For the first time that day, Josh glanced at me.

Noelle suddenly decided she would get an Eskimo cone. *Uh-oh,* I thought, *I hope she doesn't think I'm going after Sam.* And then I thought, *Maybe I just did him a favor! It wouldn't hurt for her to think another girl wanted him.*

Mona was in the middle of a great story about one of her basketball players, when our table fell silent. I felt Noelle slip back into the chair next to me. "Wow," she whispered in my ear. I turned to see what everyone was staring at. A bouquet of long-stemmed red roses was being offered to me.

Chapter 18

"Andrew!" I exclaimed. "What are you doing here?"

He laughed. "Surprised?"

Of course not, I thought sarcastically, *guys always show up with armloads of flowers for me!* "Kind of."

"You didn't think I'd remember your schedule, did you?" he said, smiling. "You didn't think I was listening to you when you told me about your job."

That was what why he brought the flowers — to make a point?

"This is so romantic!" said Mona.

"The only time I got flowers from a guy, they were ugly blue carnations in a stupid-looking corsage," moaned Caitlin.

"Hey, I gave you those," Jake teased, and the other guys laughed. I could tell from their laughter that they were uncomfortable. While the girls gazed admiringly at the bouquet, the guys glanced at one another—except Josh. He was watching me, his face expressionless, even more unreadable than his cool "coach" face.

"They're incredible," Noelle said. "They're like velvet. Quick, put them in my water cup. You don't want them to die."

"Is there any significance to their being eight of them?" Caitlin asked.

Andrew liked her question. "Yes, there is one for each day I've known Jamie. Yesterday was our one-week anniversary."

A *one-week* anniversary?

"That's *so* romantic!" Caitlin gushed, her cheeks pink.

"Lucky girl!" murmured Noelle.

The guys just looked at one another—except Josh, of course. They thought it was dumb. They thought it was especially dumb that the girls thought it was so wonderful.

"Excuse us, please," I said, leading Andrew away from the table. He draped his arm over my shoulder and I wanted to remove it, but I didn't want to embarrass him or me in front of the others, so I just kept walking, waiting till we got outside to ease away from him.

"Andrew, that was very thoughtful. I—I just don't know what to say."

He laughed and touched my cheek. "I've never seen you so surprised. Your face said it all!"

If surprise was the only thing he saw, then he didn't read my entire face. "It's just a little overwhelming. And I'm at work."

"That's what made it so much fun."

"Let's talk later, okay?"

He caught my face in both hands. "Looking forward to it," he said, and kissed me on the mouth.

When I got back to the dining hall, I found my roses carefully arranged in a vase the girls had borrowed from the kitchen. "We should take them to our locker room where they'll be safe," suggested Caitlin.

We looked like a group of vestal virgins or something, bearing the flowers to our locker-room sanctuary.

Mona had not said anything since that first exclamation about how romantic the gift was. Perhaps she knew that, for me, it wasn't. After setting the flowers on the bench, the four of us hurried to the driveway where the two buses full of kids would pull up.

"Pretty roses," Sam said to me as I stood next to him.

"Let's not talk about them, if you don't mind."

"I don't mind," he replied.

The kids arrived, and our third graders turned out to be enthusiastic and rambunctious. After two of them repeatedly bonked each other on the head with plastic baseball bats, and another painted the girl next to him instead of the paper in front of him, Sam observed, "God's paying me back for when I was eight."

The schedule worked well, assigning the second and third graders to sports and outside games during the first hour, the theory being to run the energy out of them before bringing them indoors. Josh and Noelle worked with their second graders on a field adjacent to ours, but the kids kept us all too busy to notice what the others were doing. Later, our groups passed twice in the hall between the lower school's art room and library. Josh and Noelle had their group walking neatly two by two, holding hands, while Sam and I looked like shepherds of a wayward flock.

"Second grade, ha! They're a piece of cake," Sam whispered to me with a wink.

By four fifteen, we were tired, the eight of us laughing and almost slapstick as we tried to get the kids on the correct buses. There were some last-minute exchanges of riders, but finally everybody seemed to be in the right place, and the yellow buses bounced over the speed bumps and headed off.

Each of us had been assigned cleanup duties and mine was to make sure the athletic equipment was back in the right closets. I had just finished and was exiting the guys' gym when Josh entered. We faced each other in a narrow doorway.

"Hi."

"Hi."

"How did it go?" I asked.

"Fine. How did it go for you and Sam?" he asked.

"Fine."

Josh looked like he was going to say something more, then changed his mind. He moved to his right and I moved to his left, which meant we both moved to the same side. Then he moved to his left and I to my right, blocking each other again.

"Which way?" he asked.

We have to get past this, I thought. *We have to break down this wall we're building before it gets too high to do anything about.* I stood in the middle of the doorway and said, in an effort to make conversation, "What kind of sports are you going to do with the second graders?"

"The usual."

"Like what?" I asked, trying to be patient.

"T-ball."

"Our third graders were wild and really fun. I want to do some soccer with them and maybe some kind of pitch-and-run game."

"Good."

"You know, Josh," I said angrily, "I'm not

that bad to work with!" The moment I blurted it out, I wished I hadn't.

The color in Josh's cheeks deepened, which confirmed that he had requested the change in assignment.

"Sam is a great guy," he said. "You'll enjoy being teamed up with him."

"Sam is interested in Noelle," I replied. "He would have enjoyed being teamed up with *her*."

"He is—in Noelle? He never mentioned that!" Josh muttered something under his breath. "Well," he added in a philosophical tone, "maybe he'll learn a few tricks from you and lover boy."

"From who?"

"You know who," Josh answered quickly. "I'm sorry, Jamie, but one lousy week makes an anniversary? Trial offers from AOL last longer than that!"

I agreed with him, but I'd die before letting him know that.

"The way all of you girls were looking at the roses and him—I couldn't believe you were so suckered in!"

"Maybe all of you guys should have taken

notes. Don't criticize Andrew just because you don't know how to romance a girl!"

I saw the hot yellow flash in Josh's eyes, the same one I had seen when I checked his shot the first day of lacrosse camp. When his eyes got that amber gleam, whether it was in anger or in the heat of a game, I was fascinated by them, and couldn't stop looking. They were hypnotic.

Josh pulled his eyes away from mine and rubbed his forehead, a gesture I was getting used to when I was around him.

"I don't *try* to give you headaches," I said.

He laughed a sharp, funny laugh. "No, you're just a natural."

"Sorry."

He took a deep breath and let it out slowly. "*I'm* sorry. Maybe the other guys and I should have taken notes. Maybe I'm just jealous at how well Andrew does it. In any case, it's none of my business."

"Look," I said, "we got off to a really bad start last week, and then I made everything worse with that stupid bet. I take the blame for really messing up things between us. But can't we put that behind us now? It'll make camp more fun for everyone. Can't we just be friends?"

Josh was rubbing his forehead again, which kept me from seeing his eyes.

"Please stop doing that," I said.

He laughed that odd laugh again, then admitted, "It shouldn't be that hard to be friends."

"We have a lot in common," I said.

"Yeah, we do."

"But you're still mad. You still don't want to look me in the eye," I observed.

His eyes flicked up to mine. "Okay, buddy, I'm looking. Now, which way are you going?"

"Let's both go to our right, and there should be room enough."

We managed to get past each other and, I hoped, beyond our past.

Mona and I walked together to Stonegate's parking lot, sharing accounts of the kids we had met that day. When we reached our cars and opened the doors to let out a day's worth of burning sun, she said, trying to sound casual, "So, will you be stoop-sitting tonight?"

"The Os are off, but that's no reason not to enjoy the stoop. Want to come over?"

"Oh, no, I don't think so."

"Ted will probably be around."

"I don't want him to think I'm chasing him."

"You're my friend, why wouldn't he think you'd come over to see me?" I reasoned with her. The truth was, I wasn't looking forward to an evening full of short, breathy sentences—full of, as my mother would say, "unspoken desire."

"Maybe tomorrow night," she said, "since I was just there Sunday."

"Whatever." I climbed in my car despite the fact that it still felt like an oven.

"Jamie," she called after me, "your roses are in the locker room. You forgot them!"

"I didn't forget," I said and drove off.

Pulling up in front of the house, I found Ted at the other end of my commute. I was pretty sure he had been waiting for me, although he tried to look as if he just happened to be there reading the biochemistry newsletter he held up in front of his face, squinting into the western sun, sitting on the blazing hot stoop.

"Hey, Jamie," he said.

"Hey, Ted, just get home?"

"A few minutes ago." He stood up. "I'm glad I ran into you."

Waiting on your steps a few feet from my steps isn't exactly running into me, I thought, *but okay.* "What's up?"

"A prof at the lab gave me four tickets for tomorrow's night game. Upper deck, but behind home plate. Want to go?"

"To see the Orioles play Boston—are you kidding?" I replied enthusiastically.

"I thought, uh, maybe your friend Mona would like to come with us."

Of course. It shouldn't have surprised me; it wasn't the first time I was a means to an end in dating. "She probably would," I said.

Perhaps my face showed too many of my thoughts, for he added quickly, "If there had only been two tickets, I would have asked just you, Jamie. But since there are four, I thought, well, maybe, you would enjoy bringing your friend—and Josh."

"Josh?"

"Aren't she and Josh friends?"

"Yeah, but—"

"I thought it would make it seem more casual, like a bunch of friends going out. I really like her, Jamie. I mean I really, *really* like her."

"I never would have guessed," I said dryly.

"Great," he replied. "I don't want to come on too strong and scare her away."

"Listen, Ted, maybe instead of Josh, I could ask—"

"Not Andrew!" he interjected.

"—someone else from camp," I finished. "And why *not* Andrew?"

Ted shifted his weight from one foot to the other, and seemed to be debating what to say. "I just don't think it would be a good idea."

Was he worried that Andrew would be competition for Mona's attention? Loyalty to Mona, as well as a strong desire not to be their messenger of love, kept me from telling him he had absolutely nothing to worry about.

"I've got Mona's phone number inside, if

you want to come in for a minute while I look for it."

"Actually, I thought you could ask her," he said.

"But you're the one inviting her."

"Do you have her e-mail address?" he asked.

"Ted, are you afraid to talk to her on the phone?"

"Yes," he answered bluntly. "I've never been good on the phone."

"Okay, I'll ask her, but just this once. Next time, you're on your own."

"And you'll call Josh, too," he said.

"Well, I'll find someone from camp."

"I think Josh would be the best choice," he called after me.

"Maybe."

I called Mona almost immediately, because if I had been in her shoes, I'd have wanted her to call me right away. Over the phone, we sorted through her entire closet, selected three outfits, narrowed it down to one, then settled on something completely different.

When I hung up, I imagined wearing a T-shirt that said "Sports Buddy" on one side, and "Chaperone" on the other. But I got over my flu of self-pity by the next morning.

Chapter 19

Mona and I met early on Tuesday to transfer her clothes for the game to my car and to squeeze in a jog. On our second mile, we came across Sam, who fell into step with us.

"Listen, Sam," I said, "my next-door neighbor, Ted, has four free tickets to the Os game tonight. He asked Mona and me, and thought maybe I could ask someone else from camp. I don't want to mess things up for you and Noelle, but if it doesn't, would you like to go?"

Sam sighed. "There's nothing to mess up," he said. "And anyway, it wouldn't hurt if she thought girls like you and Mona liked to hang out with me. But my brother and his wife are visiting with their kids—I can't duck out. Why don't you ask Josh?"

"Do you know if anyone else here likes baseball?"

"Why don't you ask Josh?" Mona repeated Sam's question.

"Because I'm not in the mood to have him say no," I replied honestly.

"I thought you two were supposed to be friends now," Sam remarked.

I turned to look at him.

"Watch the hole," he warned, and I just missed stepping in it.

"Did you talk to Josh after camp yesterday?"

Sam nodded. "He said you guys apologized to each other. So maybe it would be nice to ask him to the game."

"Except now he might feel like he can't say no," I argued. "I just don't think it would be comfortable."

"To the top of the hill?" Sam asked.

"I'm game," said Mona, and the three of us sprinted up the steep incline to the next level of fields.

"Whew!" I said.

"I'm done," Sam answered.

"I'm not. I feel like I've got so much energy!" Mona told us, running in place, popping the air with her fists.

"Soaring on the wings of love," I replied. "You go, girl."

She took off across the field. Sam and I turned toward the girls' and guys' gyms and the PE offices. "In case you didn't notice that glow, Mona's in love," I told him.

"Yeah? With who?"

"Ted, the guy with the tickets. That's what the baseball invitation is all about. Ted is trying to make the date seem like a group get-together, so he won't scare her away. The thing is, there isn't a snowball's chance in hell that he'll scare her away."

Sam shook his head. "Some guys got all the moves, like that guy who brought you the roses yesterday. The rest of us, me and your friend, Ted, act like boobs and back our way in."

I laughed.

Sam cupped his hands to his mouth. "Yo! Hotshot!" he called.

Josh, who was about to enter the guys' gym, turned around and Sam beckoned to him. He dropped his athletic bag at the door and trotted toward us. As Josh got closer, I saw the wary look in his eyes, and I knew I had made the right call in not inviting him.

"Morning," he said. "Did you go for a run?"

"A very short one," Sam replied, "though Mona's still going. Josh, do you have any plans that can't be changed tonight?"

"I do if you're trying to con me into helping you with your nieces and nephews," Josh said.

"I planned to, but Jamie beat me with a better offer—the Oriole game with her and Mona and someone named Ted."

"They're playing Boston," I said, and heard myself sounding nervous. "Schilling is pitching."

"Just so you know, hotshot, Jamie asked *me* first."

"Because I didn't want to put you on the spot, Josh," I explained.

"Don't tell him that," Sam said. "He's cocky enough as is." To Josh, he said, "She's willing to take second best."

"For Mona's sake," I added quickly. "I mean,

we're doing it for Mona's sake, not that you're second best."

"Mona's in love," Sam filled in.

"With Ted—Ted Wu?" Josh asked.

I nodded. "She met him Sunday. Ted took one look at her and *wham*! Then she looked back, and suddenly it was like the Mona we all know had left the premises. It was amazing. I don't believe in love at first sight, but I swear, I expected to see the fat little guy with the bow and arrow hovering around."

"And did you?" Josh asked, smiling a little.

"No. Anyway, now they're both panting shyly—"

Josh raised a questioning eyebrow and Sam laughed.

"You know what I mean, panting for each other, but acting shy, and so Ted wants to go out with her in a casual-friends kind of situation, though I don't know who he thinks he's fooling. He's gone straight off the deep end—I find it totally unbelievable."

"Apparently you haven't read enough of your mother's books," Josh said.

"So it's settled," Sam declared. "I'll leave you guys to figure out the details." He headed toward the gym and, being suddenly alone with Josh, I felt awkward.

"Listen, if you don't want to go, it's okay," I assured him.

"I'd like to go," he said. "It's Schilling versus Lopez, isn't it?"

"It is," I replied, relieved, "and Lopez has been fabulous lately."

We walked together to where the path split between the two gyms, talking about baseball. It seemed as if I really had gotten myself a new guy-friend and sports buddy.

That morning I had a blast with my basketball players. Mona and I paced our girls through drills and let them do half-court four-v-fours, then had a full-court scrimmage between our two teams. I watched the beginning of a player's true understanding of how she should position herself, and realized why my father found this work so satisfying; I also saw the beginning of friendships and, inevitably, the start of a clique. I think a lasso would have helped me handle my Energizer Bunny. I had to bench Camille for a little talk, but when I put her back in for the last ten minutes, she played brilliantly.

At twelve fifteen, we gathered at the same table as yesterday, though we were no longer divided up as girls on one side, guys on the other. Just as we sat down with our food, Ms. Mahler arrived and told us that the storyteller we had promised to our second and third graders wasn't showing up. The big M was obviously annoyed. "People think, because it's a free summer camp, that they aren't required to keep their commitments. We need to keep our commitments to *these* children more than any."

She said the lower school librarian had come in and selected books for us. Noelle, Josh, Sam, and I picked up our lunches and followed Ms. Mahler to the lower school. The librarian had also left a key to a closet full of costumes and props. As we sat on the miniature chairs at a short-legged table, we chose the tales we wanted to do and decided who would read each part, then we sorted through the closet of theatrical stuff. Sam started getting silly and put on a Goldilocks wig. Every time Josh laughed at his friend, I noticed it—felt it—maybe because I still found it surprising.

At one o'clock, Sam and I collected our kids from the bus and played a version of soccer that should have been called Mob Ball; wherever the ball rolled, so did a mob of kids. Even the goalie kicked a goal at the *other* end of the field. After wearing out the kids and taking a water and bathroom break, we went inside for art. I don't know what it is about glue, but I have never escaped an arts-and-crafts class without getting things stuck to me.

"Do you want me to tell you that you've got macaroni on your butt?" Sam whispered, as we shepherded our flock to the library.

"Left side or right?"

"Both."

I reached back with both hands and brushed myself off, which disappointed several third graders who had been waiting to see if I'd crunch when I sat down.

The sweet little second graders were thrilled to be in with the big third graders, and our third graders were just as delighted to show off in front of the younger kids. It took some effort to seat them on the library floor and quiet them down, but once the stories began, the kids entered a whole different zone. Their favorite tale was Little Red Riding Hood.

Noelle came skipping onto our makeshift stage area in a red cape with a hood that framed her face so perfectly I thought our fearless woodsman—Sam—might jump into the scene to save her a bit too soon. Sam, however, stayed with me off to the side, seeming glad for an excuse to stare at her.

Enter the Big Bad Wolf. Josh prowled across the stage, wearing tall gray ears and a long tail that was attached to his belt loop in the back.

"Oooo," breathed the campers.

He grinned wickedly, smacked his lips, and cocked his head one way, then the other, studying his audience as if choosing his dinner. One of the kids hissed at him.

"So many arms and legs, so little time," said Josh, as he continued to prowl and eye the kids. Noelle skipped past him, pretending she didn't see him.

"I'm very hungry," said Josh. "And I love

little ears, and little noses, and sweet little toes and fingers."

The kids wriggled with pleasure and a fun kind of fear.

"Thumbs are tough, though. They're way over-developed, ever since Game Boy. I never eat thumbs."

Some of the kids held up their thumbs, showing them off.

"Well, well, well," Josh said, eyeing Noelle, "here comes a tender morsel. I'm going to hide."

Josh crouched behind a chair, where he was anything but actually hidden, and Noelle skipped toward him.

"No, no, go back, go back!" the kids cried. "There's a wolf!"

I was amazed to see that my toughest customers had totally bought into this bit of pretend.

Noelle turned around, as if she were listening to them. "I guess I'll take the long route to Grandma's."

Now Josh stood up, hands on his hips. He glowered at the kids, who happily hissed back at him. Then he assumed a different pose. Swinging his tail, like a lifeguard swinging a whistle, he strutted his stuff, making his move toward Noelle. The kids just giggled, but Sam and I were leaning against the wall, doubled up with laughter.

"I told you he was cocky," Sam whispered to me.

"Oh, little miss Red Riding Hood," Josh called, his voice arching upward. He called her three times, then finally said, "Yo, Red!"

Noelle turned. "Is that a friendly voice I hear?"

"No, no! It's a wolf!" screamed the kids.

But this time, Little Red Riding Hood wouldn't listen to their advice. She told the wolf exactly where she was going. And when he advised her not to hurry, but to stop and enjoy the flowers along the way, she did just that. The wolf, wiggling his fingers with eagerness, scooted toward "Grandma's."

Scene two: Dressed in somebody's old flannel-and-lace nightgown with a frilly dust cap on my head, I stretched out on a library table. I placed a blanket on my legs, laid back, and pretended to snore. Josh rapped on another table, and I sat straight up.

"Who's there?"

"It's me," Josh answer in a high-pitched voice, which made the kids squeal. "Little Red Riding Hood."

"Little Red Riding Hood? Oh my dearest, my sweetest, my loveliest—"

"That's me," Josh said.

"Come in, come in!"

He peeked around an imaginary door.

"Why," I exclaimed, squinting at him, "Little Red Riding Hood, how big your eyes have grown."

"The better to see you, Grandmama."

"Why, Little Red Riding Hood, how big your nose has become."

"The better to smell you, Grandmama."

"Why, Little Red Riding Hood, how big your mouth is."

"The better to eat you up!" Josh shouted and rushed through the imaginary door.

I guess it was instinct. Just as he reached me, I hopped off the table. He came around it, and I faked him out with my best basketball move and went around to the other side. We inched back and forth, the table-bed between us.

"You little brat," he said—to me, not Grandmama.

"What makes you think that Grandma gave up without a fight?" I hissed back. Then I turned and hurdled a chair. The kids hooted and hollered as he chased me around the library.

When I passed Ms. Mahler sitting by the back door, I thought, *Oh God, I'm in for it.* I raced up to the staging area, dodging chairs left and right, and finally let Josh catch me. One moment, he had me by the forearms, the next moment I was in the air. In one quick motion he had picked me up and flung me like a sack over his shoulder. I hung head downward and beat my hands against his back. The kids cheered.

"Hey," I hollered at them, "you're not supposed to cheer for the Big Bad Wolf." But they didn't care. They applauded loudly as he carried me off to the costume closet.

"You're a lot of trouble, Grandma," he said, as he dumped me on a pile of clothes, but when I peeked at him through the nightgown that he was helping me pull off, he was laughing. Together we yanked the gown down over his square body. When I transferred the dust cap from my head to his, arranging it over his wolf ears, he looked so ridiculous, the white ruffles framing his face and pink lace around his neck, I couldn't help it, I laughed and laughed and could barely stand up.

"Is something funny?" he asked, not cracking a smile, but his eyes dancing with that golden light.

Then "Grandmama" scooted out to the bed, hopped up on it, and pulled the covers to his chin. The kids howled at the sight of him dressed up like that, and Little Red Riding Hood had to take a moment to get her composure. Even the big M, sitting back by the door, was giggling.

Red and Wolf ran through the big eyes, big nose, and big mouth lines, then the wolf pounced. Red didn't put up a fight, but the woodsman sure did. The kids ate up every

moment of the hammiest struggle ever per-
formed on stage. While Josh and Sam clashed,
Josh threw his dust cap, then his gown "off
stage," as we had arranged at our lunch meeting. I grabbed them, put them on, and waited
for Sam to pursue Josh to my side of the stage.
Sam cornered Josh, but it took some work
with his cardboard ax to finish him off, especially since Josh decided to rise twice from the
dead. Finally, he flopped back, and I, dressed as
Grandmama, stepped over his body. "Ta da!"

"Oh, Grandmama! You're alive!" Noelle
cried, flinging her arms around me.

"Ow!"

Josh had bitten my ankle, then quickly
flopped on his back again.

The applause was thunderous, as thunderous as it gets with little second- and third-grade
hands, then Ms. Mahler stood up and gave a
shrill blow of her silver whistle. "Buses, children, we must get you to your buses."

I glanced at the clock. We were ten minutes
over.

Sam in his Robin Hood "woodsman" hat,

Noelle in her red cape, me in my nightgown and cap, and Josh in his ears and tail, herded the kids outside.

"Nice outfit, girlfriend," Mona said to me. Her fifth graders were already in their bus seats.

"You ought to see Josh in it."

Once the kids were boarded, Ms. Mahler turned to the four of us. There was a tiny smile on her face. "You made my day," she said.

Chapter 20

At six P.M., Mona and I were sniffing every bottle and tube in my mother's bathroom collection.

"Too fussy," I said, twisting a cap closed and slipping the tube back on the shelf, "way too fussy."

"How about this?" Mona held a bottle beneath my nose.

"Ooooh!"

"Want some?" she asked, as she dabbed it on herself.

"No, no, we can't both smell like you, Mona. If he likes it, that has to become your scent, something he connects with you, something that you leave behind on his shirt collar and drive him crazy with."

"You've been reading up," she said. "I suppose I should write down the name."

"See if he likes it first. Do you think it's okay to wear this necklace—"

"It's gorgeous on you, you had better wear it."

"I mean, since it's from Andrew and . . ." my voice drifted off. It was mine now, wasn't it? It's not like he owned my right to wear it. "We should get down there," I said. "The guys have been here for more than five minutes and who knows what my mother is entertaining them with."

My fears were fulfilled. As we entered the room behind the living room, my mother was showing Ted the outline for her current book, and Josh was reading the Post-its and scraps taped to the wall near her writing chair.

"That's really interesting, Rita," Ted said, and sounded truly intrigued, but then the radar that comes with love—or maybe it was the new scent—made him turn to see Mona. If Mona had looked good in the mirror, and she did, she looked fabulous now, glowing, though how that was possible in a room with little natural light, I didn't know.

Ted was looking pretty hot himself. "Hi," he said. "I'm glad you could come tonight."

He was so sincere, my mother got the same look on her face that she gets when watching a mushy scene in a movie.

Meanwhile, Josh was riveted to whatever he was reading on the wall. I walked over to him and leaned closer to see.

> *Through endless summer days and sleepless nights, the secret flame of desire burned in him. Each accidental touch of her hand seared his skin. The lightest brush of her fingers sent heat pulsing through his loins. She was wildfire in his veins and he dreamed of her coming to him and . . .*

"Whoa! Mom!" I exclaimed.

Josh looked over his shoulder at me. Realizing how close I was, I stepped back quickly.

"Mom, do you have to leave things like this on the wall?"

She squinted a little to see what we were reading. "Well, usually, if I like a passage but it doesn't belong in a chapter, I stick it up somewhere so I can use it when the time is right. You're blushing, baby," she added.

"Thank you for pointing that out."

She smiled at Josh, then observed, "You're looking a little rosy, too."

"Let's go," I said, and grabbed Mona's arm, towing her toward the living room and the front street, where Ted was parked.

As Ted drove, Josh and I took on the job of keeping up an easy flow of conversation. I admired the way Josh slipped in little things he knew about Mona, complimentary tidbits, although she really didn't need anyone's help scoring points with Ted.

We parked in a multilevel garage and walked toward the stadium. There is something so exciting about a summer evening with a baseball crowd gathering, fans eddying around street vendors who are hawking T-shirts and hats and brightly colored pennants. We passed through

Camden Yards's tall iron gates. Inside, fans were lining up at Boog's Barbecue, which was spouting huge puffs of smoke between the renovated brick warehouse that formed one side of the stadium and the playing field.

We found our seats in the upper deck, behind home plate as Ted had promised, which gave us a fabulous view of the field. Camden Yards was built so that from home plate looking outward you saw the city skyline between left and right field. Now the orange sun, setting behind us, was gleaming off glass buildings that rose up against a purple sky.

"Wow!" I said. "Wow! What a stadium!"

Josh leaned forward in his seat and smiled at me across Ted and Mona. I had entered the row first, and Mona had scooted in behind me. Josh had to insist and finally push Ted in next, so that Ted sat next to Mona. It was amazing to me how clumsy people in love could be, although I preferred Ted's awkward moves to the smoothness of Andrew. Andrew was a little too sure of the script.

"I knew you'd like it here, Jamie," Ted said.

"Wouldn't you like to get down on that field

and run those bases?" Mona asked me, sounding like herself again.

"We could show them how it's done," I said.

"Ha!" That was Josh's comment.

We stood for the national anthem, shouted out "*O!*" for Orioles when we got to that part of the song—Ted explained that it was a Baltimore tradition—and watched the game as it settled into a pitchers' duel.

The problem with pitchers' duels is that you need to talk about them. When there are lots of hits and base running, you can jump up and down and cheer, but when two pitchers are mowing down the hitters one after another, you need to concentrate on the finer points of the game, wonder about the statistics, and talk strategy as if you, yourself, once managed a major league club. But my baseball buddy who was capable of doing that was on the other side of Mona, and they were focused totally on each other. I became bored, then irritated.

They didn't need us here, I thought. Why was I taking part in this dumb charade? I was like a freakin' chaperone. *Get a grip, Ted.*

I decided I'd better get myself clear of them

for a few minutes. "I'll be back," I said, climbing over legs and heading toward the stadium ramp.

As soon as I reached the concourse, I felt better. I bought myself a hot dog and a Coke and started watching the game on the TV mounted near the concession stand. The Baltimore announcers were discussing the pitch selection and calling up stats, and I felt like someone was finally talking to me. The fifth inning was over, and the next one started, but I didn't want to go back. *Maybe they'd think I got stuck in a long food line*, I thought.

I leaned against the stadium wall, crumpling up my foil, wondering what else to eat. The Orioles got a hit and I heard the people inside the stadium roar.

"Having a good time?"

I jumped at the sound of Josh's voice. "Oh, hi."

"I thought maybe you'd gotten lost," he said.

"No."

"Is the game any better out here?"

"Depends on what kind of game you like," I replied.

He smiled.

"They, uh, they're kind of getting to me," I admitted.

"Me, too. How are the hot dogs?"

"Great."

The stadium roared and we stopped to watch the TV screen. Men on first and third.

"Can I buy you another one?" he asked.

"No, I'm going for the ice cream, I think."

We got in line together and watched as the Orioles scored their first run and then got themselves caught in a rundown between second and third.

"What are you *doing*?!" I scolded the player.

"The third-base coach should have stopped him," said Josh. "He should have been watching him, especially since he's a rookie."

We paid for our food, and I followed Josh to a window in the concourse, where we could watch the monitor from a distance, as well as lean on the concrete wall and look out over the city. Streetlamps, the lights of row houses, and the taillights of cars on a highway curling away from the city glittered in the dusk. The Orioles played spectacular defense. Josh and I discussed the problems of small- and medium-market teams in baseball. I was totally happy. I wished I could spend the whole game out there with him.

Josh balled up the foil from his hot dog and tossed it twenty feet, landing it neatly into a trash receptacle.

"Nice shot."

"Thanks. So," he said, resting his elbows on the window, looking toward the horizon of twinkling lights, "are you a believer yet?"

"In what?"

"Love at first sight."

I leaned on my elbows next to him. "I've been thinking about it," I said. "I think that a lot of people are immediately and incredibly attracted to somebody else. It's one of those things that happen frequently. And, one time in a million, it turns out to be the real thing. One time in a billion, it turns out to be real for both people."

"Cynic."

"I'm just reporting what I see."

"Or maybe what you feel," he suggested.

"All I know is, I could never fall in love that way."

"How can you be so sure?"

I played with my necklace. "I just won't let myself. I know that there are too many things a person doesn't see right away."

"Like what?" he asked.

"Like the fact that a guy wants to make varsity football more than anything and your dad is the coach. Like the fact that a guy wants to sew up his position at tight end, and your dad's the coach."

"Burned," Josh said softly.

I didn't want his pity. "Burned once, shame on them. Burned twice, shame on me. I'm not letting it happen a third time."

"Always by jocks," he observed.

"That's who I've always hung out with — till now," I added.

"Are poets any better?"

"I haven't decided." I glanced sideways at him. "How did you know Andrew was a poet?"

"We go to the same school. He's already famous. Your Mom is a hoot," he said, changing the subject. "I like her."

I laughed. "You'd never know we were related."

"Not if you're looking at the surface," Josh agreed. "But she has the same determination as you, to do what she wants, and to do it the way she wants, no matter what anybody thinks."

I looked at him, surprised.

"Am I wrong?" he asked.

"No, I think you're right."

"You're both passionate players," he went on. "You just work at different things."

"Did you meet Viktor?" I asked, wondering what Josh would think of that situation.

"He was leaving as we were coming in."

"And?" I prompted.

Josh grinned. "He's a stud."

"I finally asked my mom. He's fourteen years younger than she is."

"Go, Rita!" Josh replied.

I played with my ice cream spoon. "I don't trust him."

"With you or with her?" he asked quickly.

"With her."

"Because of something you've seen? Because

of their age difference?"

I thought for a moment, trying to put my finger on what bothered me about him.

"Or maybe because you don't trust love?" Josh added.

"Answers B and C, plus a gut feeling. Tell me about your grandmother."

"Her name is Ellen. She is *very* tough. And kind."

"And?"

"You want to know more?" he asked, sounding surprised.

"Yes."

"She met my grandfather in eleventh grade. It was—I know you're not going to buy this—love at first sight. Which probably wasn't a good thing because she married him and got pregnant instead of finishing high school.

"He died when my mother was young, and Gran raised my mother alone. It was really a struggle because she didn't have enough education to get a good job. Then history sort of repeated itself, my mother fell in love in high school, Gran raised the roof, and my mother ran away. She finally came home with a baby—me—

and no husband. I don't remember my mother, because she headed off again right after that. Anyway, Gran raised me so strictly that all the other parents wanted their kids to hang out with me. God help me if I missed a day of school! If I hadn't decided on college on my own, she would have handcuffed me and walked me there every day. But she's really a sweetheart. And she's a total sucker for romances like your mother's."

I smiled. "A lot of people are."

"Gran has sacrificed a lot for me. It was just lucky I could get the athletic scholarship and save us some money."

"It wasn't just lucky," I said. "It was ability. It was hard work. It was exceptional talent."

He turned to look at me. "Does it feel that way to you?"

"No," I admitted. "No, sometimes I get so nervous about the whole thing, I wish I had never been offered a scholarship."

Josh nodded as if he understood.

"I tried to talk to my dad about it, but I'm his kid, he thinks I can do anything."

Josh nodded again.

"I talked to my coach and she dragged out

my stats—as if they mean anything! That was high school! I'm in a different league now."

"And so you're thinking, what if I stink? What if I've lost it? What if I never had it? What if my grades go south? What if the athletic department decides they made a huge mistake? What if a kid who didn't get a scholarship plays a lot better than I do?"

I laughed. "That pretty well sums it up."

"If you're like me, Jamie, preseason practices won't help much to settle the nerves. There's nothing you can do but hang in there till you get to your first real game."

"That's what I was afraid of," I said, although it helped just knowing I wasn't the only one who felt that way.

"If you want," he added, "I can give you my e-mail address before you take off for Maryland. If you start to get nervous or down, you can just e-mail me. Not that I have anything wise to tell you, but I've been there."

"Thank you."

"Want to take a walk and tour this place? We can stop at all the monitors along the way."

I smiled. "Sounds good."

We made the entire circle of the stadium, dawdling here and there, and returned to our seats in the ninth inning.

"Where have you been?" Mona asked me.

"We've only been gone for an inning and a half," I lied.

"Oh," she said.

I leaned closer to her. "That was a reality test, Mona. You failed."

She laughed and shrugged.

Since we had eaten throughout the game, it didn't make sense to go out and eat afterward. Mona suggested walking the short blocks to the harbor and taking a water taxi ride.

"I've been wanting to do that ever since your date with—since you did it," she revised her sentence.

We picked up the boat at the dock near the Harborplace pavilions, and Josh steered me to a section of the taxi where we wouldn't be looking directly at Mona and Ted. "They may want to kiss without us watching."

"I wish they would and get it over with," I

said. "I feel silly, like a chaperone."

"I think they're kind of sweet and romantic," he said.

"Then you've been reading your Gran's books."

"No, but I have read some excerpts, and in her books they plunge into all-out passion."

"Oh," I said, as if I had never read a romance.

"What do you read?" Josh asked, laughing. "Stephen King?"

"Sometimes."

The taxi blew its horn and slid away from the dock. I turned to watch the lights of the city slowly spin around us. The dark water was bright with neon reflections and the breeze was warm, almost balmy.

I was tired of talking—not tired of being with Josh—just tired of gabbing, and happy to ride along with him from stop to stop, watching people get on and off. The wind kept plucking strands of hair from my sagging French braid. When the boat shifted directions, I saw Josh reach up quickly to brush my hair out of his face, then he realized what it was and dropped his hand just as quickly, as if to say, no problem.

"Sorry," I said, catching hold of my hair and whisking it around to the other side of my face.

"It's not bothering me," he replied.

I leaned forward, curious, trying to see his eyes.

"What?" he asked. "What is it?"

"I was wondering what color your eyes are at night."

"The same color as they are during the day," he replied.

Still, I leaned closer.

"Unless there's a full moon, of course, and the wolf in me starts emerging. But you've seen that already."

"Your eyes are a funny color."

"Why, thank you."

"They're hazel," I continued, "but sometimes they get a gold light in them. It's a warm, golden light, except when you're angry, then it's a flash, like lightning. I saw it the first day, when I checked you and kept you from scoring."

He looked sideways at me, but under lowered lids, so all I saw were his dark lashes.

"Never mind. It was a dumb thing to wonder."

And it was an especially dumb thing to say. It sounded like I was fascinated by his eyes, or something. Which I was, but that wasn't something you told a friend. I turned my attention to the guy steering the taxi, studying him as if his job were the most interesting thing in the world. Then I felt Josh's fingers under my chin. Barely touching my cheek, he turned my face toward his and gazed into my eyes.

"Have I answered your question?" he asked after several seconds—or minutes—I was too mesmerized to know.

"Um . . . yes. Even at night, their color's, uh, like our lake in Michigan, where our cabin is, green and brown with a soft shimmer of sunlight."

He blinked, then said, "As long as I'm not getting my shot checked."

"Exactly," I replied, and turned toward the shoreline. I was glad that the taxi was approaching the dock.

We disembarked and, although Ted was the driver, Josh and I led the way back to the parking garage. I turned around once and saw Ted and Mona holding hands as they walked. I thought about the way Andrew liked to drape his arm around me. Ted probably wanted to do that, and Mona would have welcomed it, but there was something touching about the way he had simply taken her hand, the way he treated her carefully, as is she were a treasure.

Josh and I climbed into the backseat and watched Ted fumble with the CD player, try to find his parking ticket, and frown at the pulsing bell that went off because he had forgotten to buckle his seat belt. When the music came on, I recognized it, but couldn't remember the singer.

Mona turned to Ted. "That's Nat King Cole," she said, smiling. "My grandmother owns every recording of his."

Ted pushed a button and the track changed. A song I knew from a movie came on. "Mona Lisa, Mona Lisa, Mona Lisa," the guy crooned.

The air inside the car was warm and smelled of Mona's perfume. I stared at Josh's knees, which, like mine, were jutting into the back of the car seat. When I glanced sideways at him, I caught him looking at me, that is, at my neck-lace. It took all my restraint not to reach for it self-consciously. I remembered how Andrew had fingered the beads, and yet I felt Josh's eyes on my throat in a way I had not felt Andrew's fingers.

Josh glanced up and met my eyes briefly. "It looks pretty on you," he said, then turned away. "Can I put down the back window, Ted?"

"Sure."

He rolled it all the way down and let in city sounds, which mixed with the romantic music. We were silent the rest of the way home.

Chapter 21

Some mornings, usually at the beginning of basketball season, when I'm still working on conditioning, and at the end, when we play game after game in tournaments, I wake up feeling as if I have not moved an inch since falling asleep the night before. My arms and legs are made of lead; even my pinkies are heavy. Other mornings, usually when I have lots of tests or papers, I wake up with my body ready to move, but my head still deep in a dreamless fuzz, and I stumble around like a sleepwalker.

Wednesday morning, I felt as if I hadn't dreamed a dream or moved a muscle since the moment I'd laid down. For all I knew, I could have died overnight. I felt like Sleeping Beauty must have after a hundred years. Which meant

I was late for my warm-up run with Mona.

"Come on, come on," Mona urged me, having already circled the track once and antsy to take off again.

"Excuse me, but I was kept out late last night," I reminded her. "Don't expect me to be energetic, just because you're high on the caffeine of love. Why don't you do another lap while I stretch?"

Mona looked me over. "You're hurting, girl-friend."

"Uh-huh."

"Did you sleep last night?"

"Yes."

"Well, I hope you remembered to put on clean underwear," Mona said, just before taking off on her lap. "You're still wearing your necklace."

I reached up to touch it, and suddenly my mind cleared, as if a little alarm clock had gone off inside me. I remembered the way Josh had gazed at the necklace lying against my neck, the way his eyes had felt resting on me.

After several more stretches, I joined Mona

and we started one of Stonegate's cross-country routes.

"Did you have a good time last night?" she asked.

"Yeah. How about you?"

"I had a spectacular time."

"Good."

"He is so great, Jamie."

I nodded.

"The way he listens, the way he laughs."

"Yeah."

"He's funny."

"Yeah."

"He's thoughtful."

"Yeah."

"He's gorgeous."

"I know."

She stopped dead and turned to me with a pained look.

"What?" I said. "What's wrong?"

"Who are you talking about?" she asked back.

I replayed our conversation in my mind and searched for the right answer. "Uh, Andrew?"

"Are you falling for Ted?" she asked.

"No, of course not, I thought *you* were."

"You're confusing me, Jamie. The tone in your voice a minute ago . . ."

I was confusing myself, because while she was describing Ted, I was picturing Josh.

"I'm still asleep, Mona," I said. "You talk and I'll just nod."

Reassured, she started running again and I matched her pace.

But I wasn't asleep. I was in another world, an unfamiliar world. My mind kept drifting back to the night before with Josh.

Then the little clock that had beeped in my head ten minutes before suddenly rang like an all-out alarm of a security system, warning of someone breaking and entering. Circling the field where the middle school boys played lacrosse, I saw Josh. He had tossed his camp T-shirt on top of his gym bag near the sideline where we ran, and was alone on the field, running, faking out imaginary defenders, slamming the ball into the goal.

Mona must have seen my reaction. "We

could just circle the field for a while," she suggested slyly.

"Why would we want to do that?"

"To enjoy the scenery," she replied.

"I've seen a guy without his shirt before."

"Have you seen Josh without his shirt?" she asked, smiling.

"A jock's a jock."

"Not always."

Josh saw us then. He stopped a moment and nodded in our direction, his hands still cradling with the stick.

"Good morning, gorgeous," Mona called.

"Good morning, Mona," he replied. "Jamie."

I waved. I felt like a fifth grader experiencing her first crush. *This couldn't be happening to me,* I thought. *I won't let this happen to me.*

"Let's cut over to the baseball diamond, Mona."

I couldn't wait to start the morning camp, to get myself back on track. But even as I explained, demonstrated, corrected, and encouraged my girls, Josh's face kept rising in front of my eyes like a pop-up ad on a computer screen.

Oh, God, I prayed, *please don't let me be falling for Josh. Please, please don't let me be falling for another jock.*

"Miss Jamie?" my Energizer Bunny said, waving her hands in front of my face. "Miss Jamie, hello?"

"Sorry, Camille."

I stayed late to talk to some of my players, and if they had wanted to stay till one o'clock, that would have been fine with me, but their mothers eventually came for them. At twelve twenty-five, both wanting to see him and not wanting to see him, I walked slowly to the dining hall. I had lost my appetite and considered spending lunchtime somewhere else, but the trained athlete in me figured that discipline was the answer to insanity. Besides, if I didn't show up, people would start asking questions.

As I approached our table, I saw that there were already eight people sitting down. Perfect, I thought, no room for me.

"Here she comes now," I heard Sam say, and someone turned around. Andrew. He gave me a dazzling smile, a smile that, if flashed into a camera, would have made the hearts of girls across the U.S. race. But mine, perversely, beat with a dull *thud-thud*.

"You're wearing my necklace," Andrew observed proudly.

The eyes of everyone at the table went straight to it, so I assumed Josh's did, too, although I was careful not to look in his direction.

"It's beautiful," Caitlin said admiringly. "You've got good taste, Andrew."

He sat back in his chair, smiling. "It's easy to dress a beautiful girl."

Jake let out a mock "Whoa!" and Todd said, "I prefer to undress them," which made everyone laugh.

"Of course," Andrew said, smiling, "that comes afterward."

I wanted to rip off the necklace and throw it at him. What was I, his mannequin? "Andrew, could we talk outside?"

"Absolutely," he said, rising from his chair. "Don't you want something to eat? Let's have a picnic."

"Just a Coke," I said, striding toward the soda machine, forcing my legs to slow down and take smaller steps. I had to maintain some kind of dignity in front of the others. "I have a lot to do to prepare for this afternoon's camp," I told Andrew as I pulled the cold can out of its slot. "I'll walk you to your Jeep."

"Wait. Let me get a copy of the poem I brought you," he said. "It's on the table."

Poem? It was then that I saw my camp buddies holding up sheets of paper and pointing things out to one another. Andrew had brought his poetry to my camp? He had sat down and passed out his writing to people I knew? I felt like he was invading my life.

"It's a poem about you," he said, and my feet froze to the dining hall floor. I was not going within a mile of that table!

"Why don't you go gather up your poems?" I suggested. "I'll wait here."

"It's just one poem. I made copies."

Oh, God! I thought, and headed for the door. He caught up in the courtyard with the picnic tables. "Where are we going?" he asked.

"To the parking lot, remember?" I said, walking fast. "I'm sorry, Andrew, but I didn't know you were coming, and I have a lot to do."

"Shall I read the poem to you, or would you prefer to read it quietly when you're alone?"

"What's it called?" I asked.

"The Kiss."

"I'll read it when I'm alone," I said, and kept walking.

The Kiss? Whose kiss? If it was about me, was it our kiss? Our kisses were lousy, and anyway, it can't be that personal, I told myself. He wouldn't distribute copies of something that personal, not to people I worked with. But he was a poet—maybe he would. I couldn't stand not knowing.

"Let me see," I said, handing him my soda and taking the poem from him.

The Kiss

Oh, for Mount Olympus's golden apples
to capture my sweet Atalanta,
my glorious high-breasted Atalanta,
running wild through
the sylvan landscape and
Demeter's fields.
Be still, be still,

woman of my wildest dreams,
while I kiss your eyes, your ears,
then encircle your neck
with emeralds that dim
and shyly hide their light
next to those jewels of yours
that gaze at me so adoringly.
Strand by strand I let down your hair,
unloosing your gold in my hands,
releasing the heat that runs
in your veins.
My lioness, my Atalanta,
I conquer you at last
with a deep and sumptuous
and everlasting kiss.

—Andrew Hunterton Wilcox

I shut my eyes, and for a moment I think I swayed with the horror.

"I knew you'd like it," he said.

My eyes flew open and I stared at him, then glanced down at the poem. What was that line about my jewel eyes gazing at him adoringly? When had that happened? I barely recognized us as the two people kissing.

I handed him the sheet of paper and took back my Coke. "Andrew, we kissed, but this isn't anything like how I remember it."

Apparently, he thought my confusion was a literary one. "You know who Atalanta is?" he asked.

"Yes, you explained to me once before."

"And Demeter?"

"Someone who owns fields."

"She is the goddess of fertility."

"Oh. Well, that clears up all my questions. Andrew, you should *not* have shown other people this poem. It's very personal."

"As a poet, I must exploit the personal," he said, "although I know it makes it difficult for the people who share my life."

"Well," I told him, "as a camp counselor, I must check my supply of macaroni and glue, although I know it makes it sticky for the people who share *my* life. Good-bye."

"Excuse me?"

"I said good-bye. Fare thee well, or however

they write it in poetry. Do you want your necklace back?"

"No!" he exclaimed, looking angry and
bewildered. "Fare thee well? Because of one
poem?" Then his confidence returned. "I caught
you by surprise. We'll talk later."

"Trust me, you've said enough already."

I turned and headed toward the PE offices.

I didn't know what I was going to do when
I got there, but I certainly wasn't returning to
the dining hall. I could just imagine the remarks,
and I didn't know what I'd do if Josh said something. I thought about hiding in the locker room,
but I didn't want to face questions and comments from Caitlin, Noelle, or even Mona.

I sat for ten minutes inside the lobby of the
athletic department building, my head in my
hands, glad for the silence and the chance to
be alone. Then a reedy voice called from Ms.
Mahler's office, "Is everything all right?"

I sat up straight. "Uh, uh, yes."

"I left Friday's revised schedule with Mona
at the dining hall," Ms. Mahler said, remaining
behind her office door. "They thought you would
be back since you hadn't had your lunch."

"Thanks, I'll get it from her later."

There was a long silence, then some rustling, and the big M emerged. She set on the table next to me some crackers, a peanut butter jar, and a battered kitchen knife, then silently returned to her office.

"Thank you. Thank you very much," I called in to her, and munched away.

Chapter 22

I told myself that it was NCAA Finals, University of Maryland was the underdog, and I had to walk onto the court looking like I thought I could lead my team to victory. And believe me, it would have been easier to do that than to join the others at the curb where the buses deposited our campers.

"Mona," I said, pulling her aside, "do people think it's about me?"

It would have been reassuring if she hadn't known immediately what I was referring to, but she did. "Jamie, he told us it was."

I couldn't curse, not with a group of third graders swarming around me.

Sam and I walked our group of wild things to the field that we always used, next to Josh and Noelle's field, not that I was looking in their direction.

Sam touched me lightly on the arm. "If you take any more deep breaths, you're going to hyperventilate."

"I can't believe he gave out the stupid poem!" I hissed.

"I wish I had his guts," Sam replied, with a glance in the direction of the adjacent field, where Noelle and Josh were playing Duck, Duck, Goose.

"That was ego, Sam, not guts."

For the first forty minutes, Sam and I held races, athletic as well as funny ones, like hopping and three-legged, then we switched to our "skilled sport," badminton. Birdies were popping all over the place. Our second hour that day was reading and writing a group story, and our third took us back to the art room, where the kids painted self-portraits. After putting the kids on the bus, I asked Sam to switch cleanup jobs with me. I didn't want to run into Josh at the gym.

He agreed, and I hurried off to the lower school's art room, where I cleaned up the spills, wiped down paint containers, and rinsed the brushes. During the course of the afternoon, Caitlin had passed along a message that everyone was gathering at the swimming pool after work. That's all I needed, to see Josh horsing around three-quarters naked at the pool. I'd wait till everyone had changed into their suits at the locker room, then I'd grab my stuff and head home.

I watched the big black hand of the school clock inch its way over the passing minutes, then locked the art room door behind me and left. On the way out, I leaned over a water fountain—a very short one since it was in a lower school—and took a long drink. My necklace flopped against my nose and got wet. Straightening up, I caught hold of it, and turned just as Josh came through the library door.

His eyes darted to my hand and the necklace, and I immediately felt defensive.

"Why aren't you in the gym?" I asked.

"Why aren't you?" he shot back.

I hung on to the necklace like an electrocuted person who couldn't let go of a live wire. "Sam and I thought it would be good to change jobs."

"Noelle thought the same," he said.

"Oh. Well, I guess that makes sense. See you later."

I walked past him. There was plenty of room in the school hall, but it seemed to me as if he took it all up. *Just get to the door, Jamie,* I told myself.

"Some poem," he said.

I stopped. "Excuse me?"

"Some poem," he repeated. "Fortunately, your boyfriend gave out copies, so none of us had to take notes, as you suggested the last time. Now, Todd, Jake, and I know exactly how to kiss a well-dressed girl."

Embarrassment merged with anger, and I spun around. "He wasn't describing me—us—whatever!"

"Well, the necklace was the same," Josh pointed out.

"That's the only thing that was."

"I'd be willing to bet otherwise."

"How much?" I asked.

Josh blinked with surprise at the question.

"It's pretty easy to fall into a stupid bet, isn't it?" I said, making my little point.

"Five bucks," he replied.

Now I blinked.

"Backing out?" he asked.

I seethed. "Oh, I'd be willing to bet a lot more that that."

"Let's keep it at five."

"Cheap," I said, and he took a swift step toward me. Surprised, I backed against the wall.

"Losing your nerve?" he asked.

"My nerve for what?" My voice sounded shaky. He kept moving toward me. His face was four inches from mine.

"To win the bet. To prove that it wasn't a description of what it's like to kiss you."

"Win the bet—you mean by kissing?"

"How else?"

"We could ask Andrew," I said, which made no sense.

"Andrew's already told us what he thinks. It's down to *he said, she said*."

I tried to see past Josh's shoulders. I remembered how broad they were, how they felt like a protective cape the day he had pulled me back from the picket fence. And I remembered how, the longer we had played that day, the more I became aware of him, the stronger the sensations were each time we made contact. The slightest brush of his arm against mine had made me tingle. These feelings hadn't started last night. I was just too jaded about jocks and distracted by Andrew to recognize the signs last week. The fat guy with the arrow had snuck in then.

Oh, Lord, I'm in deep, I thought. *Run, girl-friend, run.* But an insane voice said, *If you don't kiss him now, you'll have lost your only chance.*

"So?" I challenged Josh. "I'm ready."

That made him hesitate.

"I thought you said you didn't need to take notes, but already you've forgotten. You start with the hair."

Josh's eyes flicked to the elastic fastener on my high ponytail. He reached around my head with both hands, as if he were going to yank the tail straight off. But instead, he examined the silky band and tried to slip his finger under its tight elastic. He tried several times and frowned. I wanted to laugh—a few barrettes and a little braiding had made Andrew's challenge much easier. The laughter died in my throat, however, as Josh attempted to painlessly remove the fastener, his face a picture of concentration, one hand inching the stubborn elastic down the ponytail, the other holding onto the hair above it so it wouldn't be pulled.

He was so careful, so gentle. By the time he had gotten the troublesome thing off and had slipped it over his wrist, I couldn't wait to feel his fingers in my hair. I was afraid he'd forgotten the next line of the poem, but he hadn't. Ever so slowly he loosened my hair and let it tumble in his hands, his eyes avoiding mine, but gazing at my hair so intently that I found myself looking down at it rippling in his fingers. I had a crazy impulse to kiss his wrists. But that wasn't part of the script.

He held my face in his hands, but still would not meet my eyes. He kissed me on the forehead. That wasn't part of the script, either; how could it be, kisses on foreheads were for children, not lovers, and yet it sent a sweet buzz zizzing through me. Just having his face that close to mine made my cheeks warm.

He softly kissed one eyelid, then the other, then slowly moved his head to one side, all the while keeping his face whisper-close to mine. With his thumb, he drew back my hair and kissed my left earlobe, then he moved his head and lightly touched his lips to my right ear. More zizzing.

One hand touched my neck and he gently slid my necklace around, moving the clasp. He carefully unfastened it and held up the beads for me to take. I gazed at the thing as if I were hypnotized. He put it in my hands and curled my fingers around it, then lowered his head, and ever so gently touched his lips to my skin, kissing me on the spot where the clasp had lain against my neck. I shivered.

His hands let go of my face and hair, and I sank back against the wall, as if I had just had the most passionate, all-consuming kiss in the world. How could that be? Was it the way he kissed, or the fact that it was Josh who was kissing me? I had a bad feeling that those two things couldn't be teased apart. I had a doomed feeling that it all came back to Josh, and no one else in the world could do it like him, not for me.

He rested his hands against the wall, his palms flat and supporting him, so that not one bit of his body touched mine, although he was just two inches away and every millimeter of my skin felt his presence like an intense heat.

Tilting his head, he let his lips brush mine once . . . twice . . . three times.

Kiss me! I wanted to scream, but I got control of myself. I swallowed hard, then I took a deep breath and said, "That's not how Andrew and I kiss."

"So you're admitting the poem was a description of him kissing you."

"I'm not admitting anything," I replied, wanting only one thing, the kiss—or whatever it was we were doing—to continue.

His mouth touched mine and this time stayed longer. Oh, God, what sweetness there was in such a simple kiss! Where did he get this magic? And why didn't he put his arms around me? If he didn't soon, he was going to find me on the floor—both my knees were ready to give out.

But now his lips were returning to my eyelids and my ears.

You've done that part! I wanted to say, except I really didn't want him to stop. I wanted this bet to go on forever.

He brushed his lips over one cheek, then the other, and I caught his mouth with mine, unable to stand too much more wandering. There was such purity in his kiss, tears burned in my eyes.

Then I felt his arms around me, his hands on my back. I realized I had been standing there with my hands almost limp by my side. I had no idea what I had done with the necklace. I raised my arms and slid them around Josh's neck.

He stopped kissing me then. I pulled my head back slightly to look at him. I really wanted to see his eyes, that golden shine in them, but he wouldn't meet my gaze. His eyes were trained on my mouth and I thought he was deciding whether or not to continue.

Don't stop! I thought. I pulled him toward me and pressed my mouth to his in a way that would have made the fictional Andrea and Brad shout, "You go, girl!" I heard Josh's quick intake of breath as his arms tightened around me. I felt a delicious shudder run the entire length of us.

I didn't know who was holding up who as

we kissed. We let go at the same time, both of us staggering back against the wall. A long silence followed, during which I tried to figure out how to breathe normally again.

"So," I said at last.

"So," Josh replied.

I peeked sideways at him. Did he have any idea how he had just rocked my world, how he had changed all that I thought was possible? I wondered how I was going to walk down the hall and out the door in a straight line. Maybe that's what Melanie meant when she talked about bringing a guy to his knees. At the moment, mine felt totally unreliable.

Then Josh reached in his pocket and pulled out a five-dollar bill. "You were right," he said, "the poem doesn't describe your kiss. Andrew must have been fantasizing."

I stared at Josh with disbelief, stared down at his hand forcing the money in mine. My fingers closed around the bill and squeezed it hard, like the way his words had just squeezed my heart. How could two people kiss, one feel a major earthquake, and the other just a tremor? I watched him as he strode down the hall and out the door. He wasn't having a bit of trouble walking in a straight line, I noted, as my knees slowly buckled and my back slid down the wall, till I was sitting on the floor.

Chapter 23

Wednesday night, I wished for the deep and dreamless sleep of the night before, but it was impossible. When I did sleep, I dreamed of Josh; and the rest of the time I tossed and turned and heard Andrew's words in my head: "All last night, I lay in bed thinking of you, dreaming of you, longing for you—" *What goes around comes around*, I thought, and I knew this wasn't going away any time soon.

I would go to college, graduate, get a job coaching at Stonegate, and eventually take over Ms. Mahler's job, living out my life as a single woman dedicated to my students and players. I would make it my special job to distribute crackers and peanut butter to girls who ask guys,

"Can't we just be friends?" and then stupidly fall for them.

Oh, the self-pity was flowing.

At six A.M., I told myself to get a grip. I arrived at Stonegate right on time for my morning run with Mona. I had taken an extra-long shower, eaten a healthy breakfast, and thought I was looking pretty good.

Mona studied me as we did our stretches. "Did you sleep last night?"

"I sleep every night."

"What's wrong, Jamie?"

"Nothing."

How do you tell a friend who is blissfully in love that you think heart surgery may be the only answer for you?

"Jamie, what's wrong?"

"Nothing much, really. It'll pass." *In about a hundred years,* I thought.

"You don't want to talk about it?" she guessed.

"Maybe some time later, okay?"

"No problem." She gave my ponytail a yank. "I just don't like to see my friend unhappy."

We finished stretching, did a lap of the track, then Sam hailed us from the baseball diamond.

"So, is either of you interested in going out Friday night?" Mona asked as the three of us ran together.

"Uh, well, I'm not sure what I'm doing then," I replied.

Tuesday night, I had made a vow to my satin rose that I would not go out with Ted and Mona until they started acting normal.

"Me, neither," said Sam. "I'm trying to decide between the three girls who are begging to go out with me."

Mona and I turned to him at the same time, and he laughed.

"Sam, you're a catch," Mona said. "Noelle will see that sooner or later."

"Then it's going to have to be later," he said. "I asked her out Friday night, and she already has a date."

"Oh, I'm sorry," I said.

"That doesn't mean anything," Mona assured him. "Lots of girls go on dates they don't really want to go on, right, Jamie?"

"True," I replied. "We all fake it some."

The three of us chugged up a hill. "I don't think this is one of those times," Sam said. "Caitlin told me the date was with a guy Noelle has been interested in since forever and ever."

"That can't be right," I answered. "You said Noelle had a steady boyfriend last year."

He lifted the front of his shirt to wipe the sweat from his face. "Maybe she was faking it with him. Maybe she's always really wanted this guy and now he's finally noticed."

We ran on in silence, rounding the tennis courts, then Mona said, "Since Noelle probably won't realize what a mistake she's making between now and tomorrow night, why don't you come with Ted and me to see the Bayhawks? They're Baltimore's professional lacrosse team, Jamie," she added. "I wish you'd both come. They're playing at Towson."

"Sounds fun. How about asking Josh, too?" Sam suggested.

"Already did. He's busy."

"Well, I guess I can turn down those other three girls," Sam said, "although I hate to break their hearts."

"How about you, Jamie?"

"Sure," I told her. If I stayed home, I'd just think about Josh. And Sam would be good company.

"Do you want to ask Andrew?" Mona asked.

I saw her glancing sideways at me, looking for my reaction. Her question was a test more than an invitation.

"No," I said, then changed the subject.

Thursday's basketball camp went well. The day before, I had bumbled around, bewildered by my strange feelings. Today I knew exactly what the problem was and worked hard with my girls, fully determined to eradicate Josh from my consciousness for three hours.

"Hey, the big J's back," one of my mouthy kids observed.

The big J? Like the big M? I wondered.

"You were acting really spacey yesterday, Miss Jamie," one of my sweeter girls told me.

"Yeah, well, I'm not today, so I had better not catch you wandering out of your zone, *Camille*," I warned.

The girls laughed, and I winked at my Energizer Bunny.

Noon came too soon. Mona had gathered her things and was waiting for me at the gym door. "Lunch?"

"Actually, I packed mine today and left it in my car."

"Because you were afraid that Andrew would show up?" she guessed.

I nodded. It was a better excuse than saying I didn't know what to do about Josh and how to sit at the same table without staring at him.

"Walk me to the dining hall so I can pick up something," Mona said, "then we can get your lunch from the car and eat under the trees."

We walked, discussing our campers and their progress. I guessed that Mona was curious about what was going on with me, but trying to keep the conversation to something I wanted to talk about. I knew then that I'd do whatever I had to do to work around her romance with Ted. Monalisa was one of a kind, and I wasn't letting go of the chance to be friends with someone like her.

"I'll wait out here," I said, when we got to the dining hall door.

She returned quickly with a premade sub and two iced teas. "The trees by the parking lot are nice and cool to sit under," she told me, handing the extra tea to me. "They're pines, and the old needles make it cushiony."

"Perfect."

We walked toward the lot quietly, sipping our teas. When we were close, Mona veered toward the small grove, then stopped. I had just reached in my pocket for my car keys, and plowed right into her. Then I followed her eyes.

"Let's go somewhere else," she said, turning quickly, positioning herself like a good defenseman between me and the goal.

But I could see over her shoulder, and a hundred-something feet away, in a lovely place beneath the pines, Noelle was pulling food out of a cooler. On the big picnic blanket that had been spread beneath the cooler, Josh laid on his back, his eyes closed, looking totally content.

Mona turned me around and gave me a push in the direction from which we'd just come. "We can share my sub."

I nodded and kept looking back as we walked. I felt so stupid, so blind, so ridiculously naive. There wasn't a guy alive who wouldn't find Noelle beautiful. Unlike big-boob Melanie, Noelle was both beautiful and classy, not to mention nice. And she didn't do silly things, like hurdle library chairs.

How convenient, I thought, how very convenient I made it—what a great excuse I gave Josh for asking Ms. Mahler to change the schedule! Why had I assumed he was trying to avoid me? He had a bigger goal in mind. I was an idiot.

"I'm really sorry, Jamie."

"For Sam?" I asked, taking a final look backward.

"For you," she said softly.

"When did you know—about me, I mean?"

"I began to suspect on Monday," Mona replied, "at the meeting, when you found out the schedule had been changed. You looked so hurt."

I sighed. "Took me till yesterday morning to figure it out."

She laughed and slipped her arm around my waist.

"I can't believe how naive I am. It just never

occurred to me—Josh and Noelle. Well, I guess I'm not the only one. When you bought your sub, did you see Sam in the dining hall?" I asked.

"Yes, sitting with Caitlin."

"I don't think we should tell him what we saw."

"Well, he knows Noelle is going out with"—Mona stopped to revise what she had been about to say—"some guy on Friday night."

"With the guy she's wanted to go out with since forever and ever," I said, completing the statement for her. "But it'll be easier on Sam if he gets used to that idea first. Later on, he can deal with the fact that Noelle's dream guy is his friend and teammate."

Mona nodded. "What will make it easier on you?"

"Heart surgery. Know anyone who needs a donor?" I laughed at myself, then I swore.

"Let's look for a good place to eat," Mona suggested. "Are you hungry? Do you mind onions?"

"I love onions, but no, I'm not hungry. Of course, I didn't think I was yesterday, either, when I ate Ms. Mahler's peanut butter crackers."

"She gave you her peanut butter crackers? Jamie, those are legendary at Stonegate! Only special people are offered them. Well, the PE building is as good a place as any."

We camped out in the lobby area. When the big M returned to the building at ten minutes to one, she found Mona reading a *Sports Illustrated* and me sleeping on one of the sofas.

"Did you girls have your lunches?" she asked.

"We did," I said, sitting up quickly.

"Jamie, I finally have good news for you. We have the necessary enrollment for the extra basketball clinic week after next. Shall I sign you up for that, as well as the afternoon session?"

I didn't answer—didn't know the answer. I loved the work, but if I continued on, it would mean day after day of watching Josh and Noelle.

If Sam can do it, I can do it, I told myself. But while I would never say this to Sam, I thought he might be in love with a dream, a person he didn't really know, while I was in love with— no—while I was just starting to fall for—oh, who was I fooling—while I was in deep and hopeless with a guy who wasn't just a fantasy.

"Can you give her twenty-four hours to decide?" Mona asked Ms. Mahler.

She bobbed her head. "Margaret comes in Monday to work with the afternoon campers. Let me know by then, Jamie."

"Thank you," I said.

She glanced at the clock. "Buses, ladies. Get going."

Thanks to Mona and to Sam—his string of one-liners and my desire to keep him from guessing that something major had been discovered—I made it through that afternoon, even when I had to check in with Noelle and Josh about one of their second graders. When his group moved on to the art room, the little boy had stayed behind with a stack of dinosaur books in a cozy den he had made for himself with library chairs and pillows. I went to the art room to plead his case.

Josh looked up for a moment and went back to talking to a camper. Noelle came over to me.

"Listen," I said, "one of your lambs has stayed behind with our sheep."

She glanced around the room quickly. "Marcus."

"Yeah. He's holed up with some dinosaur books. I say we leave him there. It is a summer camp, after all, and we want them to be interested in books, right?"

"I agree," she said. "We don't have to tell the big M. And I'll handle Josh."

"Does he need to be handled?"

"When he gets grouchy, he starts talking rules."

I glanced toward him.

"But really, he's a sweet guy," she said with a lovely, lilting laugh.

I laughed, too, though my stomach was clenched inside.

I returned to the library and continued on as before, but from that point on, I could feel the tears rising in me. Having told the others I had errands to run and had to leave right after work, I held myself together till I was in my car and had driven a block south of Stonegate.

Then I pulled into a little shopping center, drove behind some buildings, and sat there bawling my eyes out.

After a while, I continued on, just driving around. I ended up going out to the mall and back, the only route I really knew, giving my eyes time to lose their redness. When I finally pulled up in front of our house, I saw Andrew's Jeep parked next door. I debated which entrance to use, since he sometimes wheeled his bike in through the back. Parking the next block up, I walked cautiously toward our house, making sure he wasn't lurking, then made a dash for our front door. I was never so glad to get inside the cool mauve, pink, and purple room with a zillion pillows. "Mom?" I called out. I could feel the tears rising in me again. Maybe even big girls needed their mothers sometimes. "Mom?"

I heard the scrape of her chair in the room behind the living room. I found her there, sitting stiffly in her writing chair, her back to me, rustling papers but not actually reading them. "Mom, is everything okay?"

"Hi, baby."

Her voice sounded strained.

"Is something wrong?"

She shook her head quickly, indicating no, but she didn't turn around.

As I crossed the room, her hands went up to her face. I gently pulled them away. Her eyes looked as red and puffy as mine had fifteen minutes ago, and there was a pile of tissues next to her laptop.

"What's wrong? What happened?" I asked.

She looked down at her hands. "I got dumped."

"Dumped? You mean by Viktor?"

"He left."

I sank down in the chair next to her. Oh, God.

Chapter 24

Thursday night, after a quiet dinner and an even quieter two hours of watching television with me, Mom finally went upstairs to take a shower. I grabbed my cell phone and headed for the basement, figuring I had till the pipes stopped singing to explain things to Mona.

"That jerk!" was Mona's initial response. "That jerk!" Then she elaborated. "That rotten, greedy, disgusting specimen of mankind."

"The thing is," I said, "I can't say that to Mom. It would make her hurt more."

"He told her he's been seeing someone else for the last *two months*?"

"Someone younger," I replied. "Talk about putting a knife through her heart."

"And he owes your mother money?"

"Thousands. He has this dream of owning his own business and was buying gym equipment. It's a good thing I wasn't here when the rental truck pulled up; he'd be wearing a piece of his Nordic Walker—permanently."

"It hasn't been the best day in your life either," Mona observed. "How are *you* doing?"

I ducked the question, which I knew was about me and Josh and Noelle. "I'd be doing better if I knew what to say to my mother. She feels hurt and foolish, and I guess she was foolish, but *he's* the one who should be ashamed. I mean, she loved him and trusted him. I kind of admire her for taking the chance. I just don't know what to say to her."

"There probably isn't anything you can say, Jamie. Just being around helps her."

"Which is the other reason I'm calling. I won't be going to the game tomorrow night."

"Do you want to bring her along?" Mona asked. "We could distract her."

"No, I think some funny videos or shopping might be better."

"I send you a big hug," Mona said.

"Just so you know, I'm not being a martyr.

I think it might be better for me, too."

"Then I send you two big hugs," Mona replied. "Did you tell your mom about Josh?"

"No. She—she has enough to deal with."

"I think you should tell her."

I didn't ask why, mostly because I figured that Mona would have a good reason, and I didn't want to hear it. Mona didn't know how it was to love a parent long-distance. You don't just throw open the door like that and start talking—at least, I didn't.

I told Mona I wanted to skip tomorrow's warm-up run, then I heard the house's old plumbing go silent. I headed upstairs just to "be around."

Seven hours and forty-five mintues, that's all I have to get through, I told myself, as I parked at Stonegate Friday morning. Anybody could do that. "Just don't look at the pines, Jamie," I muttered, as I climbed out of my car. All I'd need was to catch Josh and Noelle sneaking in a good-morning kiss.

I could avoid the pines if I took a longer

route to the girls' gym, one that ran past a parking lot used by students when school was in session. I headed in that direction, doing my best to keep my eyes on the pavement in front of me. At the edge of the student lot, I stopped dead.

Josh and Noelle's cars were parked there. Noelle was standing next to his car, and Josh was half inside it, pulling something out. To my amazement he dragged from the backseat a flowered skirt and a top—girls' clothes in a blue Hawaiian print. He carried the outfit and other things, which were stuffed in a bag, to Noelle's car. As the two of them walked together, he talked, and whatever he said made her continually laugh and throw back her dark, shimmering hair.

Then suddenly they were aware of me, both of them turning toward me at the same time. Despite yesterday's picnic under the pines, I wanted desperately to believe that something innocent was going on. Maybe I could have convinced myself of that, if both of them hadn't looked so—so caught, so guilty! When Josh saw me staring, his face colored and he quickly stuffed Noelle's clothes in her car.

I turned back toward the other lot, taking the usual route past the pines. I made myself walk slowly, but I wanted to run. Oh, God, how I wanted to run. It seemed like the walk between the lot and the girls' gym stretched for miles. I pushed through several sets of swinging doors, not stopping until I reached a bathroom cubicle. I went in, latched the door, and put my feet on the toilet seat so no one would see my legs and realize I was there.

For the next ten minutes I wasted a lot of toilet paper blowing my nose. The way Mom and I were shedding tears, I figured I'd have to pick up a case of Gatorade on the way home to restore our electrolyte balance. Regaining my composure, I washed my face and went out to the gym to shoot around and wait for my girls to come.

They arrived eager to play. In a way, they rescued me. *Maybe I'd like to teach and coach middle school,* I thought, as I worked the final session with them. The girls had made a big card for me, signing it and writing cute messages on it. I loved it, and after hugging them all good-bye, carried it with me to the dining hall. Mona had promised to save me a place next to her. Caitlin was bringing a cake to celebrate the end of the week, and I couldn't not show up.

When I arrived, I saw that Mona had pro-tectively placed me at the far end of the table, next to her and across from Sam. Josh and Noelle sat at the other end with Caitlin, Todd, and Jake in between.

"I'll explain the game to you, Caitlin," Mona was saying to her. "You won't be bored. It's really fast and exciting. Why don't you come?"

Caitlin played with the minuscule seashells she had dangling from her ears, one of her artis-tic creations.

"There are a lot of cute guys to look at," Mona added.

"Yeah, I'm going," Sam said, and every-body laughed.

Caitlin turned her usual pink, then asked, "Are you going too, Jamie?"

"I was, but something else has come up."

"Got a hot date?" Todd asked.

"That's right."

"Good for you!" Sam said. "If he's got a sister, let me know."

There was more laughter.

"Where's Andrew today?" Jake asked. "How can it be lunchtime without Andrew stopping by?"

"I'm not expecting him."

"Pay up," Jake said to Todd. "We had a little bet going," he explained to me.

"If I were you, I'd watch out for little bets," I told him quietly. "They have a way of turning on you."

Any pretension by Josh that he hadn't been listening to our conversation was blown by the jerk of his head in my direction. I met his eyes steadily, defiantly—for three seconds. I couldn't keep it up. I went back to eating my sandwich. In three and a half more hours, I'd be out of there.

The time passed by slowly, it seemed, but then suddenly the kids were on the bus and camp was over. "Which cleanup job do you want today?" Sam asked me.

"Gym," I said, figuring that Josh would continue with the lower-school library if Noelle was bored with her old cleanup task.

Josh must have followed similar reasoning, because he looked surprised when we met up at the same gym doorway where we had become "friends" on Monday.

"All done for the day?" he asked.

"Yes. You?"

"Almost."

I hadn't wanted to talk to him, but now that I was, I was going to prove to myself that I could carry on a normal conversation. "Good luck with girls' lacrosse next week," I said. "Mona told me she's going to be your assistant. She's so excited."

"She has the skills and knowledge to coach it herself," he replied. "But if it gives her some confidence to work together, I'm glad we are. Did you decide what you're going to do?"

"About continuing with camp? I won't be here next week, of course. Ms. Mahler said I could have the weekend to think about the sessions following that."

Josh nodded, looking cool and thoughtful.

I ached. I preferred anger to that cool and distancing response. "You've nearly got it mastered, that professional look," I said.

"What look?"

"That one. The same one you had two Mondays ago, when the big M told you I was all yours. You're a pro and know how to hide your feelings, but just for a second, I read your face. It was like, *Don't do this to me!*"

Josh's reply was to rub his forehead.

"Now you're doing that headache thing you do when I'm around you."

He dropped his hand to his side.

"Noelle probably has some aspirin."

"Probably," he agreed.

"I know this is none of my business," I began, then bit my tongue just in time.

Josh's eyes pinned me to the spot. "Go on."

"Never mind."

"Please," he said sarcastically, "I love it when people get into something that is none of their business."

"I think you should either be more discreet or come right out and tell Sam what's going on between you and Noelle."

"Excuse me?"

"It's kind of heartless of you, Josh. Sam's had a crush on her for a long time, and he's your teammate. Your friend! Either be discreet or be honest with him, but don't be making out with Noelle under the school pines. He might see you."

Josh stared at me. "Well, thank you for that piece of advice," he said.

"You're welcome."

Josh took a step closer. "You saw me kissing her under the pines? You were there? Why didn't you come over and say hello?"

His sarcasm sliced me to the heart. "I saw you and her . . . on a blanket," I began.

"And what was the kiss like?" Josh asked angrily, his face inches from mine. "You should be good at descriptions like that after hanging around with Andrew."

My cheeks felt like they were on fire. "I didn't wait around," I said. "I didn't need to watch and take notes. I already knew what it was like to be kissed by you."

"Damn it, Jamie!" he said, his eyes blazing. "I hate the way you turn things around!"

I lowered my head. "Me too. I hate it, too," I said, squeezing past him and hurrying off.

Chapter 25

When I arrived home that afternoon, I found my mother in the middle bedroom, the room that had been filled with gym equipment, a scarf wrapped around her head and a putty knife in her hand. "Hi. What are you doing?"

"Getting ready to paint. Filling holes and cracks." She held up a plastic container. "Spackling. It works miracles."

I wondered if it was medically approved for the heart.

"I'm going to Lowe's and Home Depot tonight to look at paint chips," she went on. "I thought we'd have an early dinner. What time are you leaving for the game?"

"I'm not going."

She dabbed a bit of gooey stuff on a nail hole,

scraped it flat with her knife, then turned to me. "Why not?"

"I don't feel like it."

"If you're doing this for me, baby—"

"I'm not. Really. I like looking at paint colors, Mom. Dad and I used to spend a lot of time at home improvement stores."

Her fingers traced the line of a crack, then she smoothed on more spackling.

"You look like you're feeling okay," I observed. "Is it, uh, getting any better for you?"

"It *will*," she replied, with a determination familiar to me. Josh was right: She and I were really alike in some ways.

"Is it getting any better for you?" she asked.

She had caught me off guard. "You mean Andrew? We're not seeing each other anymore. It's no big deal."

"I meant whoever has been on your mind—and it has never been Andrew," she added.

I bit my lip. "How did you know there was someone else?"

"Jamie, my one-hundred-percent-cotton, no-frills girl, hides a pink satin rose in her softball glove."

"Well—well, that doesn't mean—"

"I see it in your eyes."

I glanced away. "I'm not good at talking about feelings, Mom."

She nodded. "Neither was your father. And I have tried hard to keep from prying into things that are very private to you. Eight years ago, when Dad and I decided that it was best for you to be raised by him, and when I decided I couldn't live in a small town where the high school coach was more important than the mayor, I lost the privilege of asking my way into your life. I love you with all my heart, Jamie, and I'm interested in whatever is important to you, but I don't want to invade your privacy."

"It's Josh, Mom. And he's got a girl."

She waited to see if I would say anything else. I just couldn't.

"For what it's worth, baby, you've got fabulous taste."

I laughed. She set down her putty knife and gave me a shy, one-armed hug.

"Listen, your father called," she said, "about fifteen minutes ago. I told him you were going to a lacrosse game tonight, and he said to tell you that he was extremely jealous. Why don't you call him now? It's going to take an hour for me to clean up this mess and get myself fixed up. After that, if you would like dinner and an evening of excitement in the paint aisle, that would be wonderful."

"Sounds good!"

Downstairs, I pulled my cell phone from my gym bag, fixed a tall glass of ice water, and took them out to the back porch. Sitting on the top step, I pressed the button for the address that said "Cabin." The phone was picked up immediately.

"Hey, Dad."

"Jamie-girl!" he greeted me.

"How are you doing?"

"Good," he said. "Great. It's wonderful to hear your voice. How are you doing?"

"Uh, good. I just got home from camp."

"How did basketball go?"

I described my players, and as I did, my enthusiasm for coaching took over. I told him funny stories, including some of my more challenging moments with Camille.

"I wish I could have been a fly on the wall," he said, when I'd finished.

"I love it, Dad."

"So, are you going to be doing another session?" he asked.

"Well, like I said before, they're not running basketball next week and someone else is signed up for the afternoon. And we're, uh, we're not sure if we're going to have the enrollment for the following week." It was a small lie. Having just gushed about how much I loved coaching, if I decided not to do it, he'd want to know why.

"So why don't you come home, Jamie?"

"What? What do you mean, home?"

"To the cabin, to the lake, like always. It would be just you and me, and whoever comes by for a visit. Some of the football team and their dads are coming Thursday to camp out for a few days. It would be terrific if you could be here."

I was silent for a moment, picturing summers past when I was sitting at a campfire, swapping stories and jokes with the football team. It seemed like ancient history. And then

I thought, someone was missing from this scenario. "Where's Miss Matlock?" I asked.

"With her sister in Boston."

"Boston! Was there an emergency?"

"Of a sort. She said if she didn't get away from the cabin she was going to lose her mind."

"Oh." When it came to love, the Carvellis were obviously star-crossed.

"She said she might swing by for a few days later this summer. She wants to enjoy city life for a while."

"I see." Did I dare give my father advice? "You know, Dad, if you really like her, maybe you should meet her halfway. Maybe you should swing by the city for a few days. It can be really fun, especially when it's got a harbor."

"I'll think about it," he said. "In the meantime, why don't you come home, Jamie? We could have a great time. The fish are biting."

"I—I don't know, Dad. I have to think about it. I'll let you know soon, okay?"

"Sure, sure," he replied. "You should do whatever you want, sweetheart." But I could tell he was disappointed that I didn't jump at the chance.

I put my cell phone in the kitchen, grabbed my basketball, and went down to the corner of the alley to shoot. Memories of the afternoon playing Josh flashed through my mind, giving a whole new meaning to the sports expression "playing through the pain." I kept shooting, trying to figure out what to do. I had the perfect excuse now. "I'm sorry, Ms. Mahler, but my father needs me." I could disappear without another word to Josh—that would be satisfyingly dramatic! I could e-mail Mona and Ted, then see them when I returned in the fall. I could end up with the summer that I had been so mad about losing. I could show up in time to swim and hike and barbecue with the guys, just like always.

Except I wasn't sure the same Jamie would show up. Except I really loved coaching. Except there were a few things I might want to talk about with Mom.

I played another ten minutes, then dribbled up the alley, went inside, and picked up my cell phone. Glancing at the clock, I punched in the right numbers, then waited.

"Stonegate PE."

"Ms. Mahler? This is Jamie. Sign me up for that job."

I called Dad back right away, because I didn't want to keep him hanging. He asked me about coming for just the week, since I didn't have camp scheduled, but running back to Michigan seemed too much like running away. *Things will get better,* I thought, and suggested that he look into plane reservations for Baltimore. "I'll treat you to the Orioles and a pro lacrosse game."

Friday night, Mom and I looked at a million paint colors, bought some primer, then went to Barnes & Noble. She picked up a book on container gardening; I picked up Stephen King's latest. We both avoided the romance section. On the way home we stopped at Blockbuster and loaded up on silly comedies, like *Naked Gun 2 ½*. We were set for the weekend.

Saturday's forecast called for hazy, hot, and humid weather, so we spent the morning sanding and spackling the middle bedroom, which had no air-conditioning, and expanded our efforts to the long skinny hall that led to the back room. After lunch, we each holed up in our own air-conditioned spaces, Mom downstairs in the room behind the living room, and me in the jungle room. I was starting to become fond of the fake leopard-skin spread.

I stretched out in my favorite position, lying back on the bed, my bare feet up on the wall, which was accumulating footprints. With the AC whirring away, I cracked open my new book and descended into psychological terror.

Chapter 26

"Baby, are you awake?" my mother asked from the other side of the door two hours later.

"Mhmmn."

"Are you dressed?"

"Yes, I'm just reading, Mom. You can come in."

The door opened.

"Jamie—"

"One more page," I told her, my nose buried in the book. "I'm at the end of the chapter. It's really scary."

"As you can see, my daughter didn't get her legs from me," Mom said.

I turned my head, then quickly swung my feet down from the wall. "What are *you* doing here?"

Josh gazed at me without answering. Mom shook her head slightly, as if to say, "I didn't invite them." The older woman between Mom and Josh smiled apologetically. "We're sorry to disturb you. I'm getting a tour of my favorite writer's workplace. I didn't realize I'd be invading your room."

The woman had iron-gray curls, a large round face, and eyes the color of Josh's. His gran. I kept my gaze on her and away from Josh as I stood up.

"Jamie, honey, this is Josh's grandmother, Ellen Stein."

"It's a pleasure to meet you," the woman said, taking my hand in her broad one. "Josh tells me you've earned an athletic scholarship to Maryland. Congratulations! I am so proud of Josh, I know how proud your folks must be of you."

"Thank you," I said. "Thank you." I swallowed hard, remembering Josh's offer to help me get through the preseason jitters, just being a kind friend.

I wanted to burrow under the bedspread. I wondered what this room looked like to Josh, what I looked like in one of my favorite Peyton Manning shirts, a big blue tank top with his number on it, flowing over a pair of pink boxers with little ribbons on them. I knew my ponytail hung more on one side of my head than the other, and hair was falling out of both sides of the clasp, but there was nothing I could do about that now. Besides, I reminded myself, what was the point? He wasn't here to admire me.

"So, Rita, I see that you like to work facing the wall," Josh's grandmother said, noticing how my mother's desk was built into the closet area.

"Yes, since I use a laptop, I can always turn my chair around to look out the window, but sometimes I need this kind of space to focus better. Here, I live totally in the world of my characters."

"The way I do when I'm reading," Mrs. Stein remarked.

And so they went on, comparing notes as reader and writer.

Josh and I stood there awkwardly. I kept my eyes on his gran and Mom, but I could feel him there as if he were the only person in the room. I started wondering if I had made a huge mistake by signing up for more camp.

"So you *do* like Stephen King," Josh said, his voice polite, almost cautious.

"Yes."

"That's his new book, right?"

"Yes."

There was a long silence between us. My mother was showing Mrs. Stein the floor plans and photos she had used for the setting of her first novel.

"What other authors do you like?" Josh asked.

"Elizabeth George. Nora Roberts." My mind went blank. "I can't think of any others."

"The Brothers Grimm?" he suggested. "Are those yours?" He gestured to the pile of fairy tale books next to my bed.

"Yes, from when I was a kid."

Curious to see what was in the pile, Josh picked up my softball glove, which was resting on top, then noticed the bit of shiny pink folded inside the leather. He opened the glove. I snatched away the rose, moving so quickly that I caught the attention of his grandmother.

She and Josh looked at me questioningly.

"It's just a rose," I said, which certainly didn't explain the way my hand had shot out to retrieve it—to protect it. The satin rose was the only bit of real romance I had left, a sweet and sincere gesture that hadn't been ruined later on by something else. I was afraid that if Josh looked at it or asked me about it, something new would be added to the rose and its memory. I was desperate to keep its magic.

"It's pretty," said Mrs. Stein. "Is it from someone special?"

"No. Yes. Sort of."

She looked directly in my eyes as if she were trying hard to understand.

"Not really," I said.

I reached for my glove, but Josh held onto it, pulling it back a little, making me meet his eyes for a moment. As soon as Mrs. Stein turned her back to look at Mom's stuff, I said quietly, "Please give me my glove." He did and I slipped past him, aware of the exact spot where his arm brushed mine.

Outside, the stoop was sun-baked and hot, but I sat on it, hunched forward, clutching the glove and rose to my chest, shivering like I was in a freezer. The shivering stopped when I saw the door of Andrew's Jeep swing open.

He climbed out and grinned. "Looking for me?"

"No, just sitting outside for a few minutes."

Andrew studied me, perhaps guessing from my appearance that I had fled some kind of scene. "Viktor isn't back, is he?"

"No. I didn't know you knew his name."

Andrew smiled. "I was home Thursday for the big fight—we're at the end of prime landscaping season, and I got off early. You should have been here for it, Jamie. It was better than a soap opera."

I imagined the scene could have won a Daytime TV Emmy, but I didn't like his joking about it.

"Does your mother already have another boyfriend?"

"No. Josh—Josh Hammond—and his grandmother are here. She wanted to meet my mother—she's a big fan of her books," I said. "One of Rita's millions of readers."

Okay, the millions-of-readers part may

have been an exaggeration, but I wanted to let him know: Rita Carvelli didn't have to hand out her writing for free at a school dining hall.

"More likely they're here because of Ted's phone call," Andrew replied.

"What call?"

"I heard him talking to Josh. He said that Mona told him to keep quiet, but he was worried about you and your mother. He told Hammond about the fight, and said you seemed very upset."

I shut my eyes for a second. I realized now what had happened. Mona had known I was upset about Josh and thought it best for Ted not to call him. Being a loyal friend, she probably didn't tell him why. Ted got worried and called Josh, anyway, and Josh had found an excuse to pay us a visit and make sure everything was okay.

It was thoughtful of Josh. It was touching. It was enough to make a grown girl bawl.

"Jamie," Andrew said. "We haven't talked since Wednesday. I was giving you some time to cool off and think things through."

"Think what things through?"

He laughed. "There was such fire in your eyes that day! You were magnificent!"

"I wasn't trying to be."

"That's precisely why I'm falling for you," he replied. "You're so real."

"The problem is," I said quietly, "I'm not falling for you."

His eyes narrowed. "You're still angry."

"I'm not. I'm just not falling for you, okay? I don't want to date you. I don't want to hurt your feelings, but I don't know how to make it any clearer."

"It's Hammond, isn't it?"

"What?"

"I saw the way he looked at me when I came to your camp."

Like you were acting absurd? I wanted to reply, but instead I said, "Andrew, listen, you have all the moves. They just don't do anything for me. You need a different girl."

He shook his head slowly from side to side. "I thought you were different, Jamie," he said. There was a tone of grave disappointment in his voice. "But you're like all the other everyday girls, turned on by a stupid jock."

Now I was mad. "I'll tell you what really turns me on—a guy who is there for other people—not a guy who assumes other people are there for him!"

Andrew frowned. Perhaps the concept was too simple for his great mind.

"I have your necklace inside. Let me get it," I said.

"Keep it! It's a trinket. It's worth nothing to me, monetarily or otherwise. Perhaps you never realized how much money my family has."

"I had a suspicion," I said. "And I'm glad to keep the necklace," I added, thinking of the way Josh's hands had felt when he freed me of it. "In a strange way, it's worth a lot to me."

"I don't understand you."

"I know," I said, and Andrew stomped inside the house.

Barefoot, with just my softball glove and the rose tucked under my arm, I walked down to The Avenue. I felt better than I had for weeks, for months. Oh, I still hurt something awful over Josh, and I knew there were going to be times at camp when I'd wonder how I'd survive it. But now, seeing my own reflection in the shop windows, I felt surprisingly comfortable —surprisingly happy—with myself.

Chapter 27

Saturday evening, right after dinner, Mom started writing, and I could hear from the click of the keys that she was on a tear. Mona dropped by. She had called earlier and asked me to join her and Ted for a movie.

"Ask me again next week," I said, as I walked her to the door. "I'll want to by then. And by the way, girlfriend, you look totally glam tonight. Poor Ted doesn't have a chance."

I waved as the two of them drove away—Ted's seatbelt alarm going off—then rested back against the steps, stoop-sitting. It was a sultry Saturday night, and down on The Avenue, neon glowed and people strolled by. Every once in a while, I'd see a pair of lovers walking slowly.

I was glad I was spending the summer

here. I felt hopeful for Ted and Mona, and excited about coaching. I was glad to be around Mom. But oh, how I ached! How can you love someone and sit alone on a summer night in the city, and not ache? What I would have done to make him want to be with me.

I closed my eyes and rested back on my elbows. Inside the house, I heard a sudden burst of laughter. Mom was laughing again — at her own story or at one of our videos — it didn't matter. *We are getting better,* I thought.

Then I heard the screen door open behind me.

"Hey, Mom."

She didn't reply. I heard the door close, then something landed softly in my lap. I opened my eyes and looked down. The rose.

"Next time, when you're asked if someone special gave you that rose, say yes."

I didn't turn around — didn't breathe — I couldn't. What was Josh doing here? Why had he come back? I picked up the rose, touching one worn satin petal with the tip of my finger.

A second rose landed in my lap, a matching rose. . . . No, *the* matching rose. I stared at it, confused for a moment, then spun around.

"Hi, Hon," he said.

I gazed in disbelief at Josh wearing a tall red wig, green cat's-eye sunglasses, and a feathery boa.

"Josh?"

"Girl, these heels are killing me," he said, then kicked off the pink mules. "Mind if I sit down?" He crouched next to me on the steps, then removed his wig and slipped off the boa.

"You?" I said, gasping for air. "You're my Baltimore Hon?"

"I left my leopard-skin pants and blouse at home—didn't want to get too many catcalls between Waverly and here."

My head was reeling. "You—you're my Hon?"

"I have to tell you, girlfriend," he said, removing the glittering sunglasses, "my grandmother was wondering what the heck you were doing with the rose from her old hat."

I glanced down at the roses in my lap. "I can't believe it!"

"She knew I lost a bet and had to dress up. She even found the shoes for me. But the roses in my hair, that was a last-minute bit of inspiration. When I split a seam putting on my outfit, Sam found the roses in her sewing box."

"Sam!"

"Yeah, we thought you'd recognize him from the HonFest, since he wasn't in drag that day, but I guess the fact that there was a whole group of guys from the team, you didn't really notice."

"I can't believe it!"

"Believe it," he said. "Jamie, try and believe. Love at first sight isn't just a fairy tale. Some people do fall head over heels—or in my case," he added dryly, "over the street curb."

I dropped my head into my hands.

"This afternoon, when Gran asked you about the person who gave you the rose, and you looked uncertain, I thought maybe I still had a chance."

With his hand, he gently lifted my face toward his. "Would you give me a chance?"

"A chance?" I echoed.

"That's all I'm asking for."

"A chance?" I repeated in disbelief.

"I've been taking notes. I've learned a few

tricks in the last two weeks."

"You're asking me for a chance? I am so freakin' in love with you!" I burst out, then, realizing what I had said and how I had said it, buried my face in my hands again.

"Are you?" Josh's voice was soft and full of wonder.

I raised my head and saw the gold light shimmering in his eyes.

"Oh, Jamie," he whispered, and wrapped his arms around me, pulling me tight against him. I loved the way he felt, the strength in his fingers, the roughness of his cheek. He started kissing me and kept on kissing me till I was breathless. Then he laughed, his deep, wonderful, intoxicating laugh.

"I don't understand," I said. "I thought you were with Noelle. I thought you couldn't stand me. What went wrong—how did it just go right?"

"I think it all started when Ms. Mahler assigned you to my team," he said. "You were right—I didn't want you on it—but you imagined the wrong reason. Jamie, think how it was for me. After laughing all season at guys who fell for girls and couldn't keep their minds on the game, I take one look at you and make a total ass of myself in front of my teammates. I spend all Saturday and Sunday thinking of you, thinking of nothing but you, wishing I'd had the nerve to leave my phone number with the rose. The next morning, I pull myself together and go to work. Ms. Mahler calls me over because she has a problem: You.

"I think I'm hallucinating, but I snap out of it when you try to sneak in a guy's stick, then check my shot." He laughed.

"Jamie, of course I didn't want to be your coach! I was supposed to be watching your footwork, when all I wanted to do was admire your legs. I was telling you to drink water, and all the while wanting to kiss that little trickle running down your neck. You were making me crazy!"

"I—I didn't think I could do that to a guy," I said.

"After work, I kept busy so I wouldn't think of you, running errands for Gran, like getting the autograph that I had totally forgotten after seeing you at HonFest. And who answers the door? You—in that sexy red thing!"

I laughed.

"I couldn't resist playing basketball with you."

"That's when I first"—I searched for the words—"noticed, when I first felt . . . when I became really aware each time we touched."

"Was it?" he asked softly, then the golden light in his eyes flashed hot. "And out popped good old Don Juan. Or Lord Byron—wasn't he the stud poet who wrote 'Don Juan'?"

I shrugged. "I should know after all the lit lessons I've had lately."

"He made it clear that you were going out with him. Good, I told myself, it's better to know she's taken. I was back in control on Thursday morning—until you told me about the bet."

"I'm sorry. I really am sorry."

"You so nicely explained that the reason you were betting Melanie and jeopardizing my job is that they had challenged you to seduce me, and I *wasn't* your type."

"I was determined not to fall for a jock."

"When you took Hannah's job, I didn't know

how I was going to get over you, seeing you all the time."

I rested my hand against his cheek. He turned his face to kiss my palm.

"When I introduced you to Sam at lunch, it was obvious that you didn't remember him. I made him swear not to tell you that I had been the Baltimore Hon."

"He kept your secret."

"He kept a bigger one," Josh replied. "He figured out why I had gotten the assignments changed and told me I should fess up—he even asked Noelle to switch cleanup jobs with me so I'd end up at the gym after camp and could talk to you alone."

"That sneak! And here I am thinking he's naive."

"Sam is naive only about himself," Josh said. "Anyway, any chance of admitting my feelings went down the tube when Lord Byron showed up with the bouquet. I gave you one old satin rose, and he shows up with eight long-stems. I didn't know how to deal with it. We got into an argument, and the next thing I knew you were asking me if we could just be friends."

The dreaded words. I closed my eyes and rubbed my forehead.

"I see the headache is contagious," Josh observed.

I laid my head against him. It was pure happiness to be resting against his chest. "So that's why, when I invited Sam to the baseball game, he kept pushing me to ask you."

Josh nodded. "Sam and Ted—two unlikely guys to be matchmaking."

"Ted?"

"He called me this morning, telling me he was worried about you and Rita. Since Gran has wanted to meet your mother, I figured it was a good excuse to show up and make sure you were okay.

"When I got here, when I looked at you, it was torture. I was just trying to get through the moment. Then I saw the rose." Josh touched one of the satin flowers lying in my lap. "As soon as I got home, I called Mona and asked what she knew about it. Then I called Ted."

"I never mentioned it to them."

"Ted suddenly started talking. He thought

Andrew was the wrong guy for you, and had decided that I was the right one. Tuesday night was a setup. Oh, he was really nervous about asking Mona out, but he had also figured that the best way to get you and me out together was to convince us that if we came, we would put Mona at ease."

"And I thought *he* was naive. That leaves just me, the last one to figure things out."

Josh smiled. "Mona hadn't. She was ready to crown me Stupid Jock of the Year."

And dump you in her pond of princes, I thought. Aloud I said, "Caitlin told Sam that Noelle had a date Friday with a guy she had been wanting since forever. And then I saw you under the pines with her."

He laughed. "That was a classic."

"It wasn't funny to me," I replied, and was surprised to find how close to the surface those tears still were.

"Oh, Jamie, I'm sorry," he said. "I know you didn't see me kiss her."

"No, I left before that. You were lying there, looking so content."

"I was sound asleep. I had been losing a lot

of it over you. By afternoon, when Noelle got to work with me, I was really grouchy. She got tired of it and chewed me out on Wednesday, then, on Thursday, tried to help me with lunch away from the dining hall. I never got lunch, I just slept."

I wanted to laugh, but the pain was still too fresh to me; all I could do was wrap my arms around him and hold on tight.

"Oh, baby," he said, and not in the way my mother did.

I tried to keep my voice steady: "When I saw you giving back her clothes on Friday morning . . ."

He pulled back and looked at me. "You thought we had been together? Jamie, no!" he said, pulling me against him. "No, no, no!"

"But the expression on your face—you looked as if I had caught you."

"Because I thought you had. I thought you'd figured out that I was the guy from HonFest. Noelle's sister had lent me the clothes, but I was too bulky for them. I was finally returning the outfit."

"But our kiss," I persisted. "You said it wasn't anything like Andrew's poem. You just walked away after it. Just walked away!"

"Andrew's poem didn't leave my hands shaking. Andrew's images didn't make me feel like my heart was about to explode. His words didn't make me feel like the world was caving in on me because you weren't really mine to kiss. I had to get away—it hurt so bad!"

I pressed my face against Josh's chest. One by one he kissed away the tears. He kissed both eyelids and traced my mouth with the tip of his finger.

"I love you, Jamie. God, how I love you."

Chapter 28
June, one year later

"Comfy?" I asked, lying on a blanket with Josh, on earth made soft by pine needles.

"Mmmm," Josh replied.

"I love it under these trees."

"Mhmmn."

"I love holding you close."

"Me too," Josh said softly.

"I get so turned on when you read organic chemistry."

"Me too," Josh murmured, then suddenly raised his head from where it had been resting on my stomach. "What?"

I laughed at him.

He closed the book and turned his head to kiss me on the tummy. I stopped laughing when his kiss traveled up my arm to that special place on my neck.

"We have a meeting to go to," I reminded him.

"I'm in an important one now," Josh replied, his lips targeting that one place on my neck, teasing me.

"You know what happens when you kiss me there," I said, sounding a little breathless.

"That's why I'm kissing you there."

I wrapped my arms around him, happily giving in, and heard *him* getting a little breathless, when a car turned into the lot near the pines. I sighed. "It's probably Ms. Mahler."

"Don't worry. She and I are a thing of the past."

"Josh!"

He laughed and rolled off of me.

We were waiting for the first meeting of Stonegate's summer camp. Most of us had come back for another year, but some things were going to be different. Mona was coaching girls' varsity lacrosse. Josh was spending mornings at Hopkins, having switched his major to pre-med, and needing to hunker down on the toughest courses when he wasn't playing lacrosse. Noelle was traveling, heading to Greece with her boyfriend and his family—no, not the guy she had been waiting to go out with since forever; that had lasted two weeks. And not the guy after him. After a while, Mona and I had lost track of all her boyfriends, but anyway, she wasn't returning to camp.

Ted was working at the lab again this summer. With Mona having won a lacrosse scholarship to Duke, they were saving money for the commute between North Carolina and Maryland. I knew something that Mona didn't: He was going to show up at the dining hall next week bearing a huge bouquet of roses to celebrate their one-year anniversary. I couldn't wait to see her face.

Sam was returning and would keep Josh laughing when he got too intense about school. Todd and Jake were back, and at the last minute, Caitlin had signed on.

"Hi, guys!"

"Caitlin!" I greeted her, as she entered the

shady pines from the parking lot. "It's great to see you."

She smiled, her cheeks turning a little pink. She was wearing cool sunglasses, which she had pushed up on her head, making her red hair cascade down her back, and a shirt like the one she had made Mona, her own design.

"You're looking good," I said, "really good."

"Thanks. I got my braces off."

"Braces? I didn't know you had them."

"Because I always smiled with my mouth closed," she replied. The confidence and glow I had seen a moment ago dimmed a little, shyness taking over.

"Well, you look terrific," Josh told her. "Heard you're going to the Corcoran next year for art."

That dazzling smile again. "I'm really excited. It's like a dream come true. Listen," she said, glancing over her shoulder, "before the others come, there's something I need to ask you guys."

"Okay," I said.

"I've been thinking about it since last June.

I thought maybe I'd forget over the winter, but I didn't."

"Go on," Josh prompted.

"You won't tell anybody I asked you this."

"No, not if you don't want us to," I replied.

"Okay. This is really dumb. Even if I get the right answer, I don't know what I'm going to do about it. I mean, I know what I should do, but anyway . . ."

"Spit it out, Caitlin."

"Is Sam dating anyone?"

"Sam?"

Josh turned to me, a slow, conspiratorial smile lighting his face.

"Do you like baseball, Caitlin?" I asked. "Do you like the harbor at night and water taxi rides when everything's sparkling?"

Ah, summer in the city.

Make summer last a little longer with these other great books . . .

THRILL RIDE
by RACHEL HAWTHORNE

Megan has the coolest summer job ever, working—and living!—at a big amusement park. But it means three months away from her boyfriend . . . and three months *with* a really hot coworker. Talk about a roller coaster!

TOURIST TRAP
by EMMA HARRISON

Cassie has her whole summer planned out, and it's going to be perfect. But then a handsome summer "invader" comes to town, and all her plans start to change. . . .

Thrill Ride

by RACHEL HAWTHORNE

My cell phone rang. With my luck, it would be another boy calling Jordan. Ridiculous thought. So she had boys coming out the wazoo. Big deal. I took my phone out of my backpack, looked at the number, and smiled. My sister. I flipped it open. "Hey, Sarah!"

She groaned melodramatically. "Are you ready to come home?"

I laughed. "I just got unpacked. Too late now!"

"So what's it like?"

"I've been here only an hour, but first impressions? It's going to be totally cool." I didn't want to tell her my doubts about my roommate. Otherwise she'd start hounding me to come home. She was almost as thrilled as Nick about my coming here. According to her, I'd abandoned her in her hour of need.

"Mom is driving me absolutely crazy," she said.

"Why do you think I took this job way up here?"

"The latest is that Mom thinks my wedding dress is too daring for church. You've seen it. What do you think?"

The neckline *was* low.

"Do you have to get married in church?"

"Why didn't you say something about the neckline when I was ordering it?" she asked now.

"Number one, you were looking in a three-way mirror, so I figured *you* could see that half your boobs were showing, and number two, because it's your wedding. You should wear what you want."

"You're doing your usual exaggeration thing, right? I mean, half my chest isn't exposed."

"Almost."

"Shoot. I hate for Mom to be right."

I smiled. That was part of the reason that so much yelling was going on at the house right now. Mom and Sarah are both stubborn, convinced that her way is the only way. For Sarah to even hint that Mom might be right was major.

"So what are you going to do?" I asked.

"Guess I'll see about changing out the gown, except that my one and only sister abandoned me for Canada—"

"I'm not in Canada."

"You might as well be. Just cross the lake and you're there."

"Do you have any idea how big Lake Erie is? It's like looking out on an ocean. You can't see the other shore."

"That's not the point. The point is: you're there, so far away. How can I go shopping for a gown without you to help me make a selection? You're my maid of honor. Maybe you could fly home for the weekend."

I laughed. "Sarah, I had to sign a blood oath that I would ask for only one weekend off all summer. And I plan to take it when you get married."

"That sucks. You being there sucks. I never thought I'd say this, but I miss you, Megan. What were you thinking when you took a job so far away?"

"I was thinking it would be a lot better than a summer of listening to you and Mom fight all the time."

"What's it really like there?"

"I'm not sure yet. Ask me tomorrow."

"Okay. I gotta go. Love ya."

"You, too."

I hung up. I sometimes thought that the reason that Mom and Sarah fought so often was because they were so much alike. Headstrong, determined, bossy. I was more like Dad: laid-back, quiet, didn't let too much bother me. Which was the reason that I'd thought I wouldn't have much trouble adjusting to living with someone I didn't know.

And maybe Jordan wasn't that bad. I mean, she'd realized that she needed to pick up her mess and she'd done it . . . almost. It could work between us.

I went back to unpacking. I didn't have that much. My clothes went into the closet or in the dresser beside my bed. My toiletries went into the bathroom. I didn't think our suite-mates were slobs, but four girls, two sinks, one counter did make for a lot of clutter. My laptop went on my desk where the DSL connection would keep me connected to the world. I put a few odds and ends on shelves nailed to the wall over my desk and placed my alarm clock on my desk next to the computer so it was near my bed for easy reach.

I looked at my watch. It was already seven. The sun was setting. I thought about calling Nick, but I guess I was being a little stubborn, hoping he'd call me.

This was insane. I grabbed my phone, slipped it into the pocket of my cargo shorts, along with my key, and headed out the door.

Outside I sat down on the sand, drew my legs up to my chest, and wrapped my arms around my knees. I hadn't expected to be homesick after just one day.

I took my cell phone out of my pocket and willed it to ring. Now I was being as stubborn as my sister, but I guess the truth was, Nick had hurt my feelings a little bit. I mean, here I was going on an adventure, and he didn't want to share it with me.

Not the actual coming here. I really did get why he couldn't just pack up and leave his job.

But when I'd gone shopping for the things I'd need, like new clothes, he had no interest in going with me. When I researched on the Internet to figure out how inconvenient it would be not to have a car, he didn't care about my findings. It was like Thrill Ride! or anything to do with it was totally off-limits, as far as a topic of conversation.

"This sucks big time," he'd said last night.

We were sitting in his car in my driveway. He'd taken me to dinner at Outback to celebrate my birthday.

"Let's not say good-bye tonight," I said. "Take me to the airport in the morning."

"Why? It's just putting off the inevitable."

"But it's more romantic at an airport."

"I don't see how. I wouldn't be able to go to the gate with you because of all the security stuff. We'd have to say good-bye outside the metal detectors. What's romantic about that?"

I'd sighed. "Well, then, I guess we'll say good-bye now."

"Yeah." He'd put his arm around me, drew me up against his side. "I'm sorry, Megan. It's just that I had plans for this summer, plans that included you and me, getting really close." He touched his forehead to mine. "You know?"

And I did know. He'd been pushing for us to take our relationship to the next level, but I wasn't ready yet. I mean I loved him, I was sure I did, but right now I was happy just kissing and snuggling.

I angled my face for easier access and kissed him. His arms tightened around me.

"God, I'm going to miss you, Megan. I don't know how I'll survive."

That's what a girl wanted to hear. Deep devotion. But it was only three months, and not all at once. I'd be back halfway through the summer for the wedding. And didn't absence make the heart grow fonder?

"Do you have to go?"

"You know I do. I gave them my word."

And that's when he started to sulk. It suddenly got really cold in the car, a drop in temperature that had nothing to do with the air surrounding us, and it frightened me a little to think that I might lose him, but it also frightened me to think that I was making my decisions based on what was best for Nick, rather than what was best for me.

"Nick, it's only for the summer."

"You don't even act like you're going to miss me."

"Of course I'm going to miss you."

I was already missing him. It was like he'd gone away from the moment I'd first told him about my summer plans.

Maybe that's the reason I was now sitting on the shores of Lake Erie feeling lonely. We hadn't kissed good-bye. We'd barely *said* good-bye.

This was supposed to be a fun, exciting excursion. I didn't want to feel guilty about being here.

Bad news. I did.

Tourist Trap

by EMMA HARRISON

Lola and I were about to turn down our regular path when I heard the sudden roar of an engine—it sounded like a chainsaw starting up or a boat revving to life. Lola whinnied and I whipped my head around, looking for the source of the noise. Suddenly a blur of red and black shot right out of the woods in front of us, into the meadow.

Clouds of dust kicked up, temporarily blinding me as Lola reared back and raised her front hoofs. I coughed and blinked my stinging eyes, gripping her reins with one hand while patting her neck with the other. It was an automatic reaction, trying to calm her down even though *my* heart was pounding from the shock. If Lola got spooked and took off, it wouldn't be good for either one of us.

Finally I felt all of Lola's feet hit the ground.

She steadied and I was able to wipe my hand across my eyes. Through the watery blur, I saw a bobbing, helmeted head atop an ATV, circling around the center of the meadow and heading back in our direction. I leaned down on Lola's neck and patted her, whispering soothing tones into her ear. The ATV skidded to a stop a few feet away.

"What are you doing, you psycho?" I shouted. "You almost killed us!"

Normally, I'm not the yelling kind, but my adrenaline was up and my pulse was pounding in my ears. Two seconds later and Lola and I would have been maimed.

The driver ripped his helmet off and my breath caught in my throat. As angry as I was, I knew that I had never seen anyone this beautiful before in my life—at least not outside of *InStyle* magazine. The driver was about my age with sharp blue eyes and brown hair, most of which was plastered to his forehead with sweat. He had a square jaw and a tiny bit of scruff on his chin and cheekbones. Usually I would have been intimidated by the way he was glaring at me, but anger was a good look for him. He wore blue jeans, a light blue T-shirt, and a black-and-red leather racing jacket that looked as if it had been through a hurricane.

"Me!?" he shouted, standing up and tossing his helmet aside. He swung his leg over his ATV and stormed over to us. "You shouldn't even be here! You're trespassing on my property."

I laughed automatically, but then my heart sank and my throat went dry. "Your property?" I asked. "You're not—"

"Jared Kent," he said, pulling his riding gloves off.

Jared Kent. An actual Kent. The Kents were actually *here*. Donna was going to flip out when she heard about—

"And yeah, this heap of dirt is my property," he added.

Ugh! My awe and excitement was cut short just like that. Clearly the Kents were actually as obnoxious as I had always imagined. Gorgeous, I'll admit—at least this guy was— but obnoxious.

"Heap of dirt?" I replied, regaining my composure. "This is the most beautiful piece of land in upstate New York!"

"Oooh! Trees and grass! I'm so impressed," Jared said, waggling his fingers. "I can get that in Central Park, thanks."

"I knew it," I said with a laugh. "I knew you people didn't deserve to have this place."

"Excuse me?" he replied, raising his eyebrows.

"You heard me. This plot has been sitting here ignored for years and then you come out of nowhere and accuse *me* of trespassing!" I said, surprised at myself. Apparently adrenaline brought out the sarcasm in me.

"Well you are, aren't you?" he shot back.

"At least I appreciate this place!" I replied, patting Lola as she stepped sideways a bit. She wasn't much for yelling.

"Well it *belongs* to me," Jared replied. "So I think my rights trump yours."

"Typical," I said sarcastically. "It's all about who owns what. It's not like Lola and I are hurting anything riding through here. You and your ATV, however, probably just ripped up tons of grass and scared away a couple dozen animals with your little joyride." He snorted a laugh, but didn't have a comeback. I was kind of on a high-and-mighty roll.

"Who the heck *are* you, anyway?" he asked.

"Who the heck are you?" I shot back without thinking.

"I already told you that," he said.

I flushed. "Oh . . . right." So much for my roll.

Jared glanced at me, then cracked up laughing. My heart pitter-pattered in my chest, and suddenly I found myself grinning uncontrollably. Our indignation had started to sound kind of absurd—to both of us, apparently. And if anger was a good look for him, laughter was ten times better.

He's a Kent, Cassie, I told myself. *An* invader. *Get a grip.*

I sighed and dismounted, dropping to the ground in front of him. He had a couple of inches on me and had the best posture I had ever seen on a guy, holding his shoulders back and his chin up. There was a small brown birthmark next to his left eye. Totally cute. I cleared my throat and looked at the ground. If I didn't watch out, I was going to be in huge trouble here. We all knew what happened the last time a local girl found a Kent boy attractive. She became the central character of gossip for the next twenty years.

"I'm Cassandra Grace. This is Lola," I said finally.

"Lola. A pleasure," he said with a quick nod at my horse. She snorted and he grinned.

"May as well tell you now that I ride through here every morning," I admitted. "You can call the police, but they're both good friends of the family, so I'm not sure you'll get anywhere."

"*Both* of them?" Jared said, pulling his chin back. "Big precinct you got up here."

"It's just a room at town hall, but it gets the job done," I said, aware that he was teasing the town already, but chose to ignore it. It was, after all, typical invader behavior. Besides, what did I care what he thought? After this conversation I was sure I would never speak to him again. Invaders didn't talk to locals unless they were buying corn from them or paying for an oil change. Not that any of us were interested in forging deeper relationships with people who paid more money for their shoes than we did for our cars.

Jared laughed and kicked at the dirt.

"You have no idea how cool it is to meet you, Cassandra Grace."

"Cassie," I said. My heart had skipped a beat when he said my name. Damn it. "And why?"

"I thought this town was going to be full of old fogies and bores," he said. "But you are clearly neither of those."

"We have lots of people who don't fall into either of those categories," I shot back. "Tons."

Jared shoved his driving gloves into the back pocket of his jeans. "Care to prove it?" he challenged.

I glanced at my watch and smirked. Okay, so maybe this conversation was going to go a little further. But only because I wanted to wipe that superior smirk off his face.

"Love to," I said.